Echo of Hooves

Echo of Hooves

by Eleanor Jones

Cover and inside illustration: Jennifer Bell
Cover layout: Stabenfeldt A/S
Typeset by Roberta L. Melzl
Editor: Bobbie Chase
Printed in Germany 2006

ISBN: 1-933343-10-9

Stabenfeldt, Inc.
457 North Main Street
Danbury, CT 06811
www.pony.us

Chapter 1

A familiar tingle of excitement rippled through Libby Blackstock's body as she hurried across the dew-laden grass of the orchard at Holly Bank Cottage. The tingle lodged somewhere between her heart and her stomach, leaving a warm kind of glow, and she felt like shouting her happiness out loud into the crisp, early morning sunshine; for today she felt like the luckiest fifteen-year-old in the entire world. In fact, she decided if it weren't for the fact that her parents were going away the next day, life would be just about perfect.

Pushing her hands deep down in her pockets she curled her fingers into tight fists and paused for a moment, lifting her face toward the vast expanse of clear summer sky. A flock of birds, tiny black dots, moved in perfect formation across the horizon, and powder puff clouds formed magically changing patterns against a glorious background of palest ice blue.

"Yes," she announced, moving forward again with a contented sigh. "Just about perfect," and her thoughts drifted toward the day ahead. All she had to do now was finish painting the stable door and wait for the feed and straw to arrive, then everything would be ready. It just felt too good to be true and, suddenly eager to reassure herself that it wasn't, she folded her arms across her chest against the rapid beating of her heart and increased her pace, stumbling over clumps of long, wet grass in her eagerness to get to the cluster of old stone buildings that were soon to serve as her own personal stable yard. And to think that only three short months ago she hadn't even owned her own horse.

The narrow wicket gate at the far end of the overgrown orchard swung reluctantly on its hinges, making a rusty rhythmic groan that seemed out of place in the silence of the morning.

The ancient apple trees stood motionless, without even the hint of a breeze to move their branches, and beyond the orchard she could see the cottage, its mellow, comfortable cream shape looming reassuringly. Yet still the heavy silence lingered, and for one long ridiculous moment she had the weirdest feeling that the whole world was holding its breath.

When she realized that she too was holding her breath, she shook her head at her own crazy imagination and stepped through the gate with a determined smile. There was enough to do today without having strange fancies, and she wasn't about to let anything distract her. After all, Jack was coming tomorrow, there wasn't much time left to make sure everything was perfect, and she really didn't want to think of anything else.

Ahead of her, growing almost across the track that led to the stable (like a sentry, she liked to think) was one of the many holly trees from which the cottage got its name. There were holly trees everywhere. Two stood on either side of the brightly painted front door, making deep green shapes against the warm cream of the walls, and there had been one growing beside each front gate stoop, until her father decided to widen the entrance.

"Can't live in the past," he had cheerfully told her mother when she complained about his cutting them down. "I need to get my van in as well as the car. What do you expect me to do... park in the lane?"

Visualizing his cheerful smiling face, Libby suddenly realized just how much she was going to miss both him and her mother. It would be great to have her grandmother to stay, but three months was a long time.

She was almost up to the holly tree when she saw it shiver. Just the slightest ripple ran through its dark shiny leaves, but it was enough to make her slow down, and in the same moment that she realized she was holding her breath again, a harsh grating sound cut through the strange stillness of the clear morning air.

She froze in her tracks, watching the vibrant tree shudder, wanting to yell out, to scream at the noise to stop, but somehow she couldn't seem to speak. And as she reached out her hand in protest, the harsh sound suddenly died again, leaving only the trembling total silence.

When the crack came it sounded to Libby like a howl of anguish. She placed her hands helplessly against her burning cheeks and watched in mute horror as the holly tree shuddered one last time, then slowly toppled to the ground, landing on the pathway at her feet with a final desolate crash.

7

"There!" came her father's voice from beyond the rippling mass of stricken leaves, and his smiling face materialized before her. "You'd never have gotten Jack into his stable with that growing right in the pathway, would you?"

Libby heard his voice and deep down inside she understood his reasons, but every fiber of her screamed in opposition as she stared in horror at the crudely sawed off stump. And for just a moment the shining leaves seemed to rustle mournfully in a strange sharp breeze, like a thousand tiny echoes of a bygone sigh.

"It did have to go," insisted her father gently, recognizing the expression of horror on his daughter's face. "Why did they have to plant so many darned holly trees around here anyway?"

For a moment Libby just stared at him, her velvety brown eyes clouded with dismay, and he took hold of her shoulder, shaking her firmly.

"It is only a tree you know, hon," he laughed. "We could have a funeral for it if you'd like, but I don't suppose it will notice."

A breeze fanned her cheek, and way overhead she heard the clear sweet tones of a blackbird calling for its mate. Common sense settled over her in a comfortable cloud.

"Why do you suppose there are so many holly trees here anyway?" she smiled, as the stricken tree shuddered into silence. "Don't you think it just might have something to do with the name? You know… Holly Bank Cottage!"

"Ah," retorted her father. "But which came first, the cottage or the holly?"

Libby frowned and he laughed out loud.

8

"Come on, let's go and get this stable finished."

At eleven o'clock next morning Robert Blackstock heaved the last suitcase into the trunk of his car and slammed it shut.

"That's it, then," he said to Sue, his wife. "Spain, here we come."

A frown settled on her face, and she chewed on her bottom lip.

"Do you really think we're doing the right thing?"

With an exasperated sigh Robert placed an arm around her shoulders.

"Libby will be fine with my mother, you know that," he insisted. "And anyway, once Jack arrives she won't even notice that we're gone."

"But that's another thing," groaned Sue. "She has only owned her own horse for three months. Don't you think she'd have been better keeping him at Broad Oak until we get back?"

"A promise is a promise," declared Robert. "We told her when we left the city that she could have her own horse, and I promised I'd have the stable finished before we left. If it weren't for this building contract in Spain, then we wouldn't be able to afford to live at Holly Bank at all, let alone keep a horse, would we?"

Sue Blackstock, however, was not so easily reassured.

"Maybe I should be staying here," she suggested.

Her husband's jaw set into a grim line. "You deserve a vacation. I want you to come, and Libby will be perfectly fine with my mother, so no more objections, please. Look, here they are now, so let's have a smile."

9

Libby's face was bright with excitement as she skipped along beside the tiny, straight-backed figure of Mollie Blackstock, and when she saw her parents standing beside the car she waved and took hold of her grandmother's arm, dragging her along the pathway towards them.

"See," hissed Robert in his wife's ear. "My mother has only been here for half an hour and Libby has already taken her to see the new stable. She won't even miss us, you'll see."

"Now don't forget," called Mollie, recognizing the concerned expression on her daughter-in-law's face. "You are only a phone call away, and I'll call you if I have the slightest problem. Now are you sure you've got everything?"

When her parents' car finally disappeared down the lane, a lump settled uncomfortably in Libby's throat and, as she blinked back a sudden and unexpected rush of tears, her grandmother's hand settled reassuringly on her arm.

"They'll be back before you know it," she announced firmly. "Now don't you think you'd better go and get that horse?"

Libby ran along the lane to Broad Oak stables, her feet thudding rhythmically, in tune with the thumping of her heart.

"Jack's coming to Holly Bank... Jack's coming to Holly Bank... Jack's coming to Holly Bank," she repeated over and over, as if to convince herself that it really was true.

When her father had told her, only a few short months ago, that they were moving, at first she had been devastated. Not at leaving the city, or even at leaving all her friends, but at the thought of never being able to go to Greenlands Riding School again... of never being able to ride Jack Flash.

10

She was almost the only person at Greenlands who did ride the bright bay gelding, as he was far too spirited to use for most of the clients, and the threat of being sold hung over his head most of the time. Not that Jack cared. All that interested him was food and getting the better of his rider, in that order.

The day Linda Brandwood, Greenlands' owner, told her that her favorite really had been sold Libby's whole world had crumbled. For a full five minutes she had been totally desolate, and then her father had burst out of Jack's stable, his face alight with mischievous delight, and announced in front of everyone that she was the new owner. Since that amazing and unbelievable episode Libby's whole world seemed to have taken on an upward curve. Sometimes it frightened her to feel so good, as if at any moment something might happen to bring everything tumbling down around her. But for now she hugged her happiness close. Jack was coming home to Holly Bank. It was like a dream come true.

The yard at Broad Oak was deserted when Libby opened the gate and latched it carefully behind her before walking across toward the tack room. Now that the moment was actually here doubts crept in. What if something went wrong? What if Jack was ill? There would be no stable owner to fall back on, and her grandmother knew nothing about horses. Was her mother right? Should she have left Jack safely here at Broad Oak until her parents came back?

She looped Jack's bridle over her shoulder and lifted his saddle from the rack. Oh well, it was too late for regrets now, and there was no way she was going to admit defeat, no matter what happened.

As she stepped from the cool air of the tack room into the warm glare of the noonday sun a shadow fell across the concrete and she glanced around to see the dumpy, dependable figure of Mary Hunter standing just behind her.

"Well, this is it," she exclaimed and Libby nodded nervously.

Mary's weathered features cracked into a smile and her gray eyes twinkled, belying her somewhat fierce appearance.

"You'll be fine," she insisted. "And you can call me anytime if you have a problem. Honestly, I mean it."

Libby felt her confidence come flooding back.

"Thanks, I really appreciate that."

"Anyway, I'll see you on Saturday, won't I?" she called. "Or have you forgotten that you are going to help out here in return for being able to use the school?"

"I haven't forgotten," Libby called back. "I'll be here first thing, don't worry, and there's the show on Sunday, remember, so Jack and I need all the practice we can get."

As Mary's broad figure strode purposefully away Libby clutched her saddle and quickened her steps, suddenly eager to get her horse home. A flutter of excitement made her whole body tingle. It was going to be all right, and she knew it.

Jack tossed his elegant head up and down when he saw her approach, pushing his broad chest against the door, eager to be out, and she ran her hand down the silken mahogany of his neck with a ripple of pride.

"We're going home, boy," she whispered and he nudged

her roughly, more concerned with the carrot he could smell in her pocket than his own immediate future.

Her fingers fumbled as she slipped the bridle over his ears, and he raised his head, teasing her as usual.

"I don't know why you're called Jack Flash," she grumbled. "The Joker would be a much more suitable name."

He blew himself out when she fastened the girth, reaching around for a hurried nip, and she slapped him firmly on the shoulder.

"That's enough messing around, pal," she ordered sternly. "Come on, it's time to go."

Five minutes later, as she swung into the saddle in the deserted stable yard, Libby felt as if she were starting out on a whole new adventure, and she glanced around her comfortably familiar surroundings with the slightest tingle of regret.

Gertrude, the black tomcat, was basking lazily in the sunshine. Two of Mary's golden brown chickens clucked busily in the corner, and several equine heads gazed out with interest while chewing contentedly on bulging hay nets.

"We'll be back on Saturday," she told her impatient mount. He tossed his head and sidled, eager to be off, but underneath she knew that it wasn't Jack Flash who needed reassuring. As long as the food kept appearing he would be happy anywhere.

Mollie Blackstock was waiting eagerly in the driveway as Libby and Jack approached the newly widened entrance to Holly Bank, and she hurried toward them, her eyes bright with excitement.

"Why, he's huge," she exclaimed, staring up at the imposing bay gelding.

13

Libby laughed and jumped down to stand beside her.

"He's only sixteen hands high, Gran. It's just that you're so tiny."

"And you are so tall," responded Mollie, looking critically at her granddaughter. "You certainly didn't get those long legs from me, or your riding skills, for that matter."

Libby's wide mouth broadened into a smile and she took off her riding hat, flicking back an unruly lock of silky, straight black hair.

"Right, let's introduce him to his new home, OK? Come on."

Jack walked eagerly enough across the overgrown orchard, but when Mollie opened the narrow, creaking gate that led onto the pathway to the stable, he hesitated.

"Come on," urged Libby, tugging at his reins, but he balked, setting his feet firmly in front of him. She knew that stubborn expression all too well, and with an exasperated sigh she looked appealingly toward her grandmother.

"I should just give him a good smack, really, but – just because it's his first time here, mind – please, will you go and get a bit of feed in a bucket? There's a blue tub of mix in the feed room next to his stable."

Mollie hurried off to do her granddaughter's bidding and Libby sighed, looking into her horse's huge brown eyes with as appealing an expression as she could muster.

"I hope this isn't how you are going to behave in the future," she told him. "And don't expect tidbits every time you misbehave, either. This is definitely a one-time favor."

Jack simply blew through his nostrils and lifted his head

to stare intently into the bushes, as though seeing something she couldn't.

"There's nothing there," announced Libby.

When Mollie returned with a red bucket, however, he seemed to forget his fears long enough to follow it eagerly, until they reached the sawed off stump of the stricken holly tree, and then he stopped dead again, snorting loudly.

"You can't really blame him," announced Molly. "Animals are supposed to have some sort of sixth sense, after all, and holly is reputed to have special powers, you know. Some people say that it's unlucky to chop it down. I don't know what your father was thinking."

"Good thing I'm not superstitious," laughed Libby. "He's taken his saw to more than just this one. Try giving the bucket another rattle."

Mollie shook the bucket loudly and Jack flicked his ears backward and forward, and then, putting fear into second place at the scent of food, he jogged hurriedly past the holly stump.

As he paused for a moment to dive his nose into the aromatic mix, Libby found herself staring down at the shiny, vibrant leaves of the discarded tree, remembering with a lurch the strange howling sound it had made as it fell. When a sharp breeze sprang from nowhere, rippling the stricken leaves, she tried to ignore the shudder that prickled her spine.

"Come on, pal," she said too loudly. "Let's get you safely tucked in to your new home."

Chapter 2

By Saturday Libby found it hard to believe that Jack had ever lived anywhere other than Holly Bank, and she loved having him all to herself, even though it meant getting up at the crack of dawn to see to him before school.

When he'd been stabled at Broad Oak, Mary Hunter used to feed all the boarders and turn them out into the far meadow in the mornings, so Libby never even saw her horse until the evening. Now she had to muck out, feed and turn him out in the orchard, all before the school bus arrived at the end of the lane, but it was well worth it just to see his bright, eager face each morning.

Anyway, she remembered with a warm glow of delight as she rode down the drive and out into the narrow country lane, now that the summer vacation had arrived she had eight weeks to spend with him, eight whole weeks to work on his show jumping career.

The pale light of early morning sunshine lent the trees and hedges and smooth green meadows beside the lane a shimmering brightness that reflected Libby's mood, and she urged Jack into a trot, enjoying the ringing sound of iron shod hooves on tarmac. She glanced at her watch; six forty-five, plenty of time to get to the stables by seven. Her thoughts drifted toward tomorrow and the riding club show that loomed on her horizon.

As usual, when she thought about Jack's very first competition, a rush of excitement tinged with apprehension turned her mouth dry. It was one thing to practice at home where everything was familiar, but quite another to perform amid the bustle of a busy showground. How would Jack react, she wondered?... Or would they even get into the ring at all?

A memory slipped into her mind of that moment last week when they were working over some fences in the outdoor ring at Broad Oak and Mary Hunter had stopped to watch.

"He's got quite a pop, that horse of yours," the stable owner had called from her position by the gate as Jack cleared an upright. Carly Nelson and Becky Mackintosh, two of the other girls who kept horses at Broad Oak, had laughed, but Libby didn't care. She knew that Jack was still green and gangly in his canter but he could jump, he really could, she was sure of it, no matter what the other girls thought.

Carly's dad was giving them a lift to the show in the Nelson's brand new horse trailer. What if Jack misbehaved? What if he refused to load? What if he made a total fool of her?

"Think positive, Libby Blackstock," she announced in a loud clear voice. That was her mother's favorite piece of advice. "No negative thoughts now, Lib," she was always telling her daughter. "If you want to… then you will." A lump formed in Libby's throat as she thought of her parents, so very far away, and a new determination crept in.

"We *will* show them, won't we, Jack?" she told the horse who jogged and sidled beneath her. "We'll get a clear round, that's what. Then let's see Carly and Becky's faces."

When she rode into the yard Mary Hunter had already started the mucking out. Her generously proportioned body was bent over a wheelbarrow, straining to heave it up onto the muck heap and when she turned to look toward the sound of hoof beats Libby could see that her face was pink with exertion.

"Sorry I'm late," she called, but Mary shook her head.

"Oh no, it's not you who's late, it's me who's early. I'm going to pick Marcus up from boarding school this morning and it's a long drive, so I thought I'd get an early start."

Libby had not yet had the pleasure of meeting Marcus Hunter. She knew from Becky and Carly that he was sixteen years old, very good looking and a brilliant rider, but had decided to reserve judgement until she met him herself. To be honest, over the three short months that Jack had been stabled at Broad Oak, she had become increasingly fed up hearing the sound of Marcus's name. Most of the time Becky and Carly didn't seem to want to talk about anything else, apart from their two horses, of course; a lovely gray hunter, Murphy, and a bright chestnut gelding named Tango.

In fact she was so sure Marcus Hunter must be a total bighead that she wasn't looking forward to meeting him one bit, for if Becky and Carly weren't raving about him then it was his mother. Mary Hunter was always talking about her precious son with glowing pride, although to be fair, Libby realized that was probably because after his father died a couple of years ago Marcus was all the family she had left.

Mary beamed at her now as though sharing a great secret.

"You can put him in Rodney's stall," she called as Libby slipped to the ground and took the reins over Jack's head. "I've turned him out for the day and his hay net is full. Then can you start at the far end? There's Flipper, Moses and the three new boarders to do yet."

Libby worked automatically, deftly twisting and turning her fork to persuade Flipper's bed of crisp wheat straw into a golden carpet, and the elegant, steel gray gelding snorted his appreciation when she turned him loose, then sank down to roll with a satisfied grunt.

"Just look at him," exclaimed Libby as Mary Hunter appeared behind her. "Why do we bother?"

Mary laughed.

"I often think that," she agreed. "Anyway, I'm leaving now. Jenny has gone to turn some of the boarders out; she'll be back in a minute and I've done the feeds, so I'll see you later… with Marcus," she added, her face crumpling into an adoring smile. "You haven't met him yet, have you?"

Libby shrugged, splaying out her fingers and Mary gave her a knowing look before hurrying off toward the cottage at the end of the yard.

As Libby finished the last stall and pushed her wheelbarrow towards the muckheap, she saw the small, neat figure of Jenny Harris coming toward her. Jenny was one of those dedicated horsy people who work for peanuts and live for the job. She owned a bay, seventeen-hand Thoroughbred gelding, Truman, with which she competed in horse trials, and when she wasn't working at the stables she went all over the county freelance teaching.

She paused outside the tack room to twist up the lead ropes and hang the head collars on the hook inside the door, then her tanned face cracked into a smile as she looked across at Libby.

"Are you ready for that show tomorrow?"

Libby flicked back her sleek black hair in one smooth movement and frowned.

"I don't think I'll ever be ready."

"Course you will," responded Jenny. "I saw you practicing the other day. He's got a real pop, that horse of yours."

"The pop's all right, it's the rest of it that bothers me," laughed Libby.

Jenny's gray eyes sparkled with warmth.

"It'll come," she insisted. "You'll see. He's still a bit green, that's all. I'll give you a hand one day if you like… And I don't want to get paid; you do enough around here as it is."

Before Libby could reply they heard a commotion from over by the barn, a fierce banging sound that reverberated around the yard and brought a dozen startled horses' heads over their half doors.

"I bet that's Truman again," groaned Jenny, sprinting off across the smooth expanse of concrete.

Libby hesitated.

"Do you want a hand?" she called after the rapidly disappearing figure.

Jenny raised a hand without looking back.

"I'll give you a shout if I do," she yelled.

Libby waited for a moment, until the banging stopped, then she picked up the handles of her wheelbarrow and heaved its load onto the gently steaming pile.

At lunchtime, when the yards were swept and the horses dozed in relaxed contentment, Libby led Jack across the yard to the outdoor ring and swung into the saddle. For a moment she sat quite still, absorbing the sight of his sharply pointed, black tipped ears, then she reached down to give him a pat before urging him forward.

When she pushed him into trot he felt so smooth and rhythmic and balanced that her heart swelled with pride; perhaps tomorrow wouldn't be so bad after all.

"Let's see him jump," called a high-pitched voice from over by the fence, and the swelling inside her chest deflated like a pricked balloon.

Becky Mackintosh was sitting astride her dappled gray hunter, Murphy, with her usual haughty elegance. She had already qualified him for the horse of the year show, and you only had to look at the lovely horse to see how. Libby sighed and smiled; it wasn't Becky's fault, she supposed, that she was confident and attractive and successful and had a beautifully schooled show horse that seemed to be good at everything he turned his hand to – although no one could ever be jealous of Murphy, for he was one of the sweetest, kindest, most generous horses ever born.

"Well, don't expect anything special," she called over her shoulder as she urged Jack into canter.

On a whim, she stupidly turned him toward a large blue and white parallel, regretting it immediately. She was quite probably risking her horse's confidence just to impress Becky Mackintosh, and who was she, after all?

Once committed, however, she clamped her calves around Jack's heaving sides, trying to keep him between hand and leg, trying to feel the rhythm as the imposing fence loomed. He snorted loudly in time with the pounding of his hooves. She took a pull as he dived against the bridle, and then her heart was soaring like a bird's as they lifted off the ground with such power that it really felt like flying.

The adrenalin rush kicked in as he landed with a thud and twisted into a buck of pure joy, and she leaned down to pat him furiously before throwing Becky a triumphant smile.

"Well, I suppose there is hope for him after all," called Becky's best friend, Carly Nelson, as she approached from the stable yard leading her lively chestnut gelding, Tango. Libby flushed a dull red, wondering why ever she always felt so threatened by these two girls. But it was her problem, not theirs, she knew that.

"Thanks," she grinned, reining in beside them. "He is getting better; he's just a bit green, that's all."

"Well, tomorrow will tell," remarked Becky with a tight smile. "*We're* hoping to take the hunter championship."

Carly giggled as her horse spun around in a circle, his nostrils flaring and his dark rimmed eyes wide with excitement.

"Not much chance of us taking a prize for showing, is there boy?" she told the fine boned, Arab-looking chestnut. "But if we win the open jumping we'll qualify for the riding club championships."

Libby smiled, still euphoric after Jack's amazing jump.

"Well, all we want to do is get around the novice course without too much trouble," she admitted.

Becky lifted her chin and looked at Libby through lowered lids as Murphy stepped willingly forward at her command, his neck, as always, set in a perfect arch.

"One decent jump doesn't really show anything though, does it?" she commented dryly. "It might just have been a fluke."

Libby felt a rush of irritation.

"I'm not doing it again, so we'll just have to wait and see," she announced firmly.

Becky shrugged.

"Suit yourself," she said, and then reined in abruptly, her blue eyes alight with excitement.

"Oh, by the way," she cried. "I think Mary has gone to get Marcus. He finished school today."

"Big deal," retorted Libby, but her remark fell on deaf ears as the other two girls rode off around the outdoor ring, side-by-side in deep conversation. Carly reined in and half turned her mount to look back.

"We'll see you tomorrow, OK?"

"Sorry…" stuttered Libby.

"Tomorrow!" Carly reminded her with a frown. "We're leaving at eight o'clock, remember."

"I'll be here at seven thirty," promised Libby, and the other two girls went immediately back to their usual topic of conversation the (not so, in Libby's view) delectable Marcus Hunter.

When Libby went to get her bag from the tack room she was

met by the distinctive, delicious aroma of saddle soap. Jenny glanced around from the saddle she was cleaning, sponge held aloft and tanned face shiny with the heat.

"Good luck tomorrow," she said.

Libby grimaced.

"I think I'll need it."

"Nonsense," insisted Jenny. "Have a bit more confidence. Why don't you give Jack a bath before you go home? You can use the hose in the yard, and there's some really good shampoo on the shelf. Nothing like looking your best to make you feel good."

"Thanks," responded Libby. "I was wondering how I was going to manage it at home, and I am going with Carly and Becky, after all."

"There you are, then," grinned Jenny. "You don't want to be outdone, do you?"

Unable to concentrate, even on her favorite TV program, Libby was in bed by nine o'clock that night. A picture of Jack kept coming into her mind; he had looked so wonderful by the time she had bathed him and trimmed him up that Jenny had tried to persuade her to take him in the showing class tomorrow.

"He'll give Murphy a run for his money," she insisted, but Libby wasn't so sure. She didn't want to make a complete fool of herself at her first show.

After tossing and turning for over an hour she eventually slipped out of bed and went to the window, staring out across the orchard toward the stable where Jack was contentedly munching on his hay net.

For a moment she stood in frozen silence as she saw a dark shape hovering in the gateway and then, suddenly, like a shadow, it was gone. She watched for a moment more with relief flooding her veins. That is all it was, after all, just a shadow, and her crazy imagination was running wild again; her mother was always telling her that it would get her into trouble one day.

With a quivering sigh and a reassuring image of her mother's face in her mind she went back to snuggle down into the cozy warmth of her bed, to dream strange dreams of distant galloping hooves and holly trees that rustled mournfully in a strange sharp breeze.

When she half opened her eyes a couple of hours later the pale eerie light still lit up her room, and she lay in the shadows, halfway between waking and sleeping. Was that really the sound of hooves she could hear, or was she still in the dream?

Vague recollections of a shadowy figure in the moonlight drifted into her subconscious. For a moment she tried to claw herself awake, but her eyelids were too heavy and, as the moon rose to its peak on the stroke of midnight, the sound of galloping hooves became a distant echo, and the rustling holly leaves that disturbed her dreams settled into an overpowering silence as slumber reclaimed her.

Chapter 3

Libby's boots made a satisfying crunching sound in the silence of the morning as she marched along the pathway toward Jack's stable. Today was here at last. Today they were finally going to the show. A tingle of excitement rippled through her and she paused for a moment, gulping in the crisp, clear air.

The weatherman on the radio had forecast rain, but there were no gray clouds to darken the soft blue sky and only the gentlest of breezes ruffled her sleek, dark locks.

She pushed her hair back from her face with a satisfied smile. Why, even the weather was on her side, she decided. Perhaps this was her lucky day after all.

Quickening her pace she ran up the narrow path toward the stable calling Jack's name, but for once his bright, eager face was not peering impatiently over the half door. Something deep inside her stomach twisted, and she called his name again, more loudly.

"Jack…! Come on, boy."

A low whicker echoed around the stable, but the big bay

gelding stood motionless in the shadows at the very back of his stall as she fumbled with the bolt.

"It's all right, boy," she murmured. "I'm here now. What is it, what's wrong, pal?"

Her fingers felt like sausages but at last the bolt slipped free and she burst into the stable. Jack heaved one great sigh and walked toward her, nuzzling up against her chest with an unexpected display of affection.

"Hey," she crooned. "What's all this about? I'm more used to a nip from you than a cuddle."

He tossed his head, duly obliging by grabbing at her jacket, and she laughed with relief.

"So you're not quite as bad as you're pretending," she told him, pressing her cheek against the velvety warm softness of his nose while trying to dispel the vague prickle of alarm that fluttered inside her chest.

It was when she slipped the leather strap of his head collar through its large brass buckle that she first noticed dark sweat marks around his ears, and her niggling fears swelled into a lurch of dismay; she had sponged his head so carefully last night.

Leading him out into the bright light of early morning the dismay expanded inside her chest, leaving a sick feeling in the upturned v of her ribs, for mud was splattered all over his legs and belly, and his coat, so silky and clean when she left him, was dark with dried sweat. What was it… what had happened… had he gotten out in the night?

Her mind did a crazy dance as panic set in. What should she do… what *could* she do? Taking a deep breath she stared up at the soft white clouds way above her head and allowed the early morning chorus of birdsong to fill her ears. She was fine, Jack was fine, and this was just another ordinary day.

Bit by bit she checked him over, contenting herself that he was unharmed. She could go and wake her grandmother, but then what could *she* do, tell the police? And what would they say? "Perhaps you forgot to brush him last night"?

Jack looked at her, his huge dark eyes shining as he gently tossed his head, impatient for his breakfast. She rubbed the backs of his ears.

"What happened to you, boy?" she murmured as ideas swept through her mind. Could someone have taken him out for a ride in the night? Had he escaped, and some kind soul put him back in his stable? The thought was ridiculous. No, she decided, her first idea was the most likely. Someone had taken Jack out for a joy ride while she was asleep.

Vague recollections of distant hoof beats that disturbed her dreams in the night sent a shiver rippling down her spine. Who could she tell? Was it fair to worry her grandmother if there was nothing she could do? The answer came loud and clear. No, there was no one to tell. She had to deal with this herself. Beginning, she realized, with getting him ready for the show.

Jack may not have looked quite as pristine as he had the previous evening, but Libby stood back and gazed at her handiwork with satisfaction. She felt better now that the telltale sweat and mud were gone, and she tried to put her fears on hold, turning her thoughts toward the day ahead.

"At least I'm not worrying about the show now," she said out loud, patting his neck enthusiastically, and as she put on

28

the saddle and fastened the girth she realized that all her nerves about their first competition really had fled, leaving only a vague excitement.

Five minutes later she was in the saddle, going through the items in her backpack again and again in her mind. Had she remembered everything?

"Well, its too late if I haven't," she announced out loud, urging Jack forward. "Come on then pal, let's get going."

His ears were pricked before her, the sun was shining, and she settled into the rhythm of his movement, listening to the comforting clatter of hooves as they set off down the drive. And then she heard another sound, a high-pitched yell from the direction of the cottage.

Jack was only too willing to slow down at her command, and when Libby looked around to see her grandmother's slight, white haired figure by the back door her chest tightened with relief and she reined in to wait as the old lady walked carefully toward her.

"Here," cried Mollie Blackstock, stretching up to hand her granddaughter a package. "I've made you some sandwiches, and make sure you take care now."

The words were on Libby's lips, the words that would share and halve her fears. "Someone took Jack out in the night and rode him." They faded away before they were spoken, stored deep inside for a better moment. It sounded just too crazy.

"Thanks," she smiled, stuffing the package into her backpack. "I'll see you later, and I'm always careful."

As Jack walked sedately down the road with none of his usual spooking and snorting Libby's thoughts swirled around and around in her head. Perhaps she had over-exaggerated the state of him this morning. Perhaps something had upset him in the night and he'd gotten himself in a complete stress charging around his stall... but what about the mud? Her heart sank again; there had definitely been no mud on his legs after she bathed him last night… but then again she had ridden him home after that, hadn't she? Perhaps he had flicked some mud up when she cantered along the grass verge. In the back of her mind lurked the realization that the ground was very dry, but at least the idea gave her something to cling to. To believe that someone really had taken him out in the night was just too scary even to contemplate.

By the time they reached Broad Oak, after scouring the grass verges for any sign of wet ground, she had almost convinced herself. The mud *must* have somehow splattered up on the way home last night, there was no other explanation, and Jack could easily have gotten very sweaty if he was stressed in the night. Feeling lighter of heart she turned in through the front gates, and when she saw the Nelson's smart maroon and silver horse trailer in the stable yard her thoughts took a positive shift forward toward the day ahead.

"You made it."

Carly Nelson's sandy colored hair fell forward across her face as she looked up from the hay net she was filling and flicked it back impatiently, securing it with a multicolored bobble.

"I said you would," she went on. "Becky seems to think you'd chicken out."

For just a fleeting moment Libby found herself wondering if Becky and Carly had anything to do with it. Perhaps taking Jack out in the night was their idea of a practical joke. A shadow flickered across her face as she allowed the idea to settle in her mind and, noting her discomfort, Carly's wide spaced, deep green eyes narrowed.

"You are nervous though, aren't you?" she insisted. "Go on... admit it."

Libby shrugged.

"What if I am?" she responded. "Weren't you just a bit worried at your first competition?"

Carly frowned.

"I suppose so," she admitted. "But that *was* a bit different. I mean, Tango was a really good jumper when we bought her, so I expected to do well. You're just coming along for the ride."

Libby's pale complexion flushed to a dark red.

"I don't *expect* Jack to win at his first show," she announced, her voice tight with emotion. "But I do hope to get a clear round... I mean, I know that it's just a school for him, really, but everyone has to start somewhere. Why, even your Tango must have been a green youngster once."

Carly turned away and began stuffing hay into her net again.

"Well, you'd better hurry up," she remarked. "We're loading up now, and Jack has to go at the front."

Libby hurriedly stowed her tack and belongings in the front

31

of the horse trailer, but by the time she went to get Jack from the stable she had left him in, Becky was already waiting to load Murphy. She stood in the middle of the yard, one hand on her hip and her shoulders squared back, holding the immaculate gray, which was rugged and booted in matching shades of navy blue. Libby's heart sank; she hadn't thought about boots or bandages.

Becky took in their appearance with her eyebrows raised and let out an amused snort, but with a spontaneous gesture of generosity similar to the one that had prompted her offer of a lift to the show, Carly pointed toward the tack room.

"Go and have a look in my big blue tack box," she said. "It's underneath the window. There's a spare set of red traveling boots in there that will suit Jack to a tee."

Handing her the lead rope Libby flashed her a grateful smile.

"Thanks," she muttered. "I should have bought some."

To Libby's relief Jack loaded without too much trouble – that really would have been the last straw if he'd refused to walk up the ramp. He hesitated, as was only to be expected, but once again Carly surprised Libby by patiently helping to coax the nervous horse into the trailer while Becky stepped from foot to foot and spun the end of her lead rope around and around.

The burly figure of Carly's father appeared in the yard just as the horse trailer ramp thudded shut.

"That's what I like to see," he remarked with a broad smile, noting that they were all loaded up and ready to go.

"I went over to see Mary about the boarding bill and I got talking to young Marcus. Bright guy, isn't he? Lots of ambition; he'll go a long way, you mark my words."

Becky and Carly exchanged an excited glance, but Libby frowned. What was so great about this Marcus-dratted-Hunter? She wondered.

Gray clouds had scudded over the sun by the time the horse trailer rumbled across the grass to park near the ringside and, as the three girls unloaded their horses, a steady drizzle began to fall.

"Better put studs in," advised Becky. "This hard ground will be like a skating rink if this keeps up."

Libby smiled and nodded, taking her time in getting Jack ready so that the others would be gone before they realized that he didn't even have stud holes in his shoes, let alone studs to put in them.

She worked in at the very far end of the field, well away from everyone else, and as soon as she asked him to go forward Libby realized that there was something very wrong with Jack. Her biggest fear had been that he would be totally overexcited and behave like a complete lunatic at his first show. The reality was very different. He hardly seemed able to put one foot in front of the other, let alone find enough energy to jump a fence. She should have noticed when she rode him over to Broad Oak that morning, should have realized why he was so quiet, but she was just so intent upon finding a reason for him to be splattered in mud. Oh, how wrong she had been. Disappointment flooded over her as her

33

hopes and dreams came crashing down. What should she do... pull him out of the class?

"Calling class five," boomed a voice over the loudspeaker system. "Novice open jumping contestants to ring three now, please."

"That's you," yelled Carly from over by the collecting ring. "Come on, Libby, it's your class."

She was standing up in her stirrups, madly waving a red rosette.

"Hurry up."

For a moment Libby hesitated, then, suddenly decided, she dug her heels into Jack's sides and he leaped forward in surprise.

As soon as they trotted through the entrance to the ring she knew that she had made a terrible mistake. It wasn't like riding Jack at all, he just felt so... so... *exhausted*.

Tears of guilt burned the backs of her eyes as she headed him for the first fence, praying for him to try. And he did, he really did try. He tried at the second and the third and at all the rest of the fences on the course. But as he heaved himself over each one, leaving half of the poles on the ground, she knew with a horrible certainty that she had asked too much. He really was totally exhausted, and her worries about him that morning were definitely not just her imagination working overtime. Either he was suffering from some kind of virus, or else her suspicions were correct and someone *had* ridden Jack in the night... ridden him almost into the ground. And she had made the awful mistake of pushing her courageous horse way past his limit.

Chapter 4

"There's always another day," remarked Carly, as they heaved up the trailer ramp. When it closed with a heavy thud she pushed the catch home and gave Libby an encouraging smile.

"Maybe traveling just stressed him out this time."

Libby shrugged. Whatever anyone said to try and console her she knew that it was all her fault; she should have listened to her instincts. Just because she didn't want to believe that something had happened to Jack last night she had made excuses and totally betrayed him, probably ruining his confidence forever.

"Maybe he just doesn't like shows," suggested Becky, her blue eyes glinting with amusement. "Either that or he doesn't like jumping."

Libby felt a rush of anger

"That's not true," she blurted out. "I think…"

She looked up, color flooding her ivory complexion.

"I think someone might have ridden him in the night… He was just exhausted, that's all."

Becky glanced across at Carly and when she saw the look

35

they exchanged Libby's heartbeat quickened and her eyes found the floor. She felt like such a fool. How could she ever have imagined that either of these two girls might believe her story? They both obviously thought she was crazy.

They clambered into the horse trailer in silence. Libby sat as far along the seat as she could, staring deliberately out of the window, and even Bob Nelson must have noticed the strained atmosphere, for as they pulled out of the entrance he started to sing an ancient pop song in a loud, tuneless voice.

"Dad," wailed Carly. "Do you have to?"

Becky started to giggle, which made Carly's father sing even louder, and both girls put their hands over their ears and pulled faces behind his back. Even Libby found herself smiling and by the time they were halfway home she had an idea that made her feel much better. She would put a decent padlock on Jack's door and sleep with the key beneath her pillow; at least then he would be safe.

As she sank back into her seat feeling more relaxed, to her surprise Becky leaned across and placed a hand on her shoulder.

"Don't worry," she said. "You don't need to make excuses. I was only joking before, you know… Perhaps he's just a bit off his game."

Libby nodded, waiting for a sarcastic comment to follow, and when it didn't come her forehead puckered into a puzzled frown.

"Maybe," she agreed, looking down at her hands. "Anyway, at least you two won."

Becky smiled proudly and held out the silver cup she had been nursing all the way home.

"Yes," she agreed, and it suddenly occurred to Libby that she was only being nice because she no longer considered Jack to be a threat. She obviously wanted all the glory for herself… Well, she was welcome to it this time, but Jack's day would definitely come, she was sure of that.

Silence fell then as the three girls relaxed in their seats thinking about their day, and Bob Nelson concentrated upon negotiating a sharp corner that led into the lane to Broad Oak.

The horse trailer swung wide and then suddenly it lurched almost to a halt, making the girls fall forward in a helpless heap, while in the back the horses struggled to keep their feet, thrashing and banging against the partitions.

"I might have guessed," cried Becky, scrambling up to peer out of the window. "That Amy Thomas is a liability! She could have caused an accident. If Murphy has hurt himself there'll be trouble."

"It wasn't Amy's fault," insisted Bob Nelson. "I couldn't see her because of the hedge."

"No wonder, when she insists on riding such a stupid little pony as Poppy," joined in Carly. "I can't understand why she isn't embarrassed about it."

Libby just stared at the other two girls in amazement. How could they be so mean?

"But Amy loves Poppy," she blurted out. "And I know she's thirteen, but she's so tiny. I don't think she looks that bad on him."

The little palomino Welsh Mountain pony was just ahead of them in the lane, trotting eagerly along, his rider sitting tall and straight-backed as she bobbed up and down to his short quick steps.

"Come on, Libby," laughed Becky. "Her legs come right down past the bottom of his belly."

Libby frowned, her heart swelling with emotion. Amy adored Poppy, and she couldn't buy a bigger pony unless she sold him.

"Welsh Mountain ponies can carry adults," she declared fiercely. "And Amy weighs nothing at all."

Becky collapsed onto the seat in a fit of giggles.

"Yes," she agreed, wiping the tears from her eyes. "But they look ridiculous."

"And can you imagine everyone in the open class at the show today trotting around on Welsh Mountain ponies?" blurted out Carly.

When the two girls doubled up into fits of laughter again Libby scowled.

"Well, maybe Amy doesn't care," she cried in defense of the tiny dark-haired girl who trotted gaily along in front of the horse trailer, unaware of the cruel taunts being hurled in her direction.

To Libby's surprise it was Carly's dad who came to Amy's defense.

"Don't be too hard on her," he said. "I was talking to her dad just the other day, and he told me what a hard time they'd been having with her."

"Why?" asked Libby. "What do you mean?"

He swung the horse trailer around a hairpin bend before going on, and she waited for his answer.

"It's only eighteen months or so since her Mom was killed

in a car accident, and he has just met a new girlfriend. He says that she's really nice, but Amy resents her. You can understand that, really. Anyway I suppose to her Poppy feels like the only relationship in her life she can count on at the moment."

"Well she's still too big for him," muttered Carly ungraciously, but her father was too busy concentrating on the road to hear her.

Libby didn't see Amy again until they had unloaded the horse trailer and she was about to mount up for the journey home. As she placed her foot into the stirrup Jack sidled, straining to turn toward the school, and she glanced around to see Poppy approaching, his hooves soundless on the soft grassy surface.

"Hi," she called warmly; guilt flooding over her at she remembered the comments Carly and Becky had made earlier.

Amy's delicate features crumpled into a delighted smile and she reined in beside Jack.

"Are you going home?" she asked. "I'll ride down the lane with you, if you don't mind."

"Course not," mumbled Libby as she swung into the saddle. Then her eyes caught Becky's through the horse trailer window and she deliberately raised her voice.

"Come on," she said, lifting her chin and squaring her shoulders. "Let's go."

As they rode side-by-side into the lane Libby refused to allow herself to look back, but she was sure she could hear titters of laughter following their progress.

"I know that they laugh at me," remarked Amy jauntily and Libby's heart skipped a beat.

"Don't try to tell me that they don't," she went on. "I know what they're like… I've been around here longer than you, remember. They think I'm stupid to keep Poppy, but …"

She looked up at Libby, her velvety brown eyes shining with emotion.

"I couldn't ever sell him… I just couldn't. And it's not as if I'm too heavy for him, is it?"

"No you're not," agreed Libby. "And that's what I told them earlier."

"See," smiled Amy. "You did know – and thanks for sticking up for me."

They fell then into a companionable silence, listening to the moaning wind that rustled the treetops overhead and chased black clouds across the darkening sky, drowning out the ringing sound of their horses' hooves. Libby shivered, placing her hand against Jack's warm neck. What if someone came back for him again that night? A compulsion to blurt it all out to Amy, to share her awesome fear, flooded over her, and she looked down at her diminutive companion.

"Amy… I want to tell you something about Jack."

Had she spoken, or were the words still in her head?

Amy looked around, suddenly aware of her companion's silence, and when she saw the expression on Libby's face her bright features clouded over.

"Are you all right?"

Libby nodded violently, forcing out a tight smile.

"I'm fine," she insisted, pushing Jack on into a trot. "Just late, that's all… I'll see you tomorrow."

Amy frowned and closed her hands on the reins, curbing

40

Poppy's desire to follow the big bay as it disappeared around the corner in a brisk trot. The fear she had glimpsed behind Libby's forced smile sent an icy shudder of premonition rippling down her spine.

When Jack's nose was plunged deep into his feed and his hay net was full, Libby closed the stable door carefully and ran off toward her father's workshop. She saw Mollie Blackstock's tiny gray-haired figure in the back doorway as she passed by the cottage and flashed her what she hoped was a cheery smile.

"I'll be back in five minutes," she promised, waving her hand. "Then I'll tell you all about the show."

"Well, hurry up."

Her grandmother's lined face was pink with the heat of the stove, and she mopped it with a brightly checked, red and white dishtowel.

"I've made your favorite… It is your favorite, isn't it… pot pie?"

Libby felt hunger pangs grip her stomach.

"I love pot pie," she cried. "And I really will only be five minutes."

Like a gift from above, a shiny new padlock lay right on her father's workbench, and as Libby's fingers closed eagerly around it her heart did a kind of dance. It was over. She didn't need to worry any more. Relief rushed into her lungs bringing a heady euphoria, and she took a great deep breath, steadying herself against the wall for a moment before running back to Jack's stable clutching her prize.

41

When the heavy-duty lock clicked smoothly shut, securing the bolt on his half door, she slipped the key deep into her pocket, her fingers curled protectively around it.

"No one will get in tonight, boy," she told the inquisitive gelding as he rattled the shiny object with his lips and blew softly through his nostrils, a distant, faraway look in his eyes.

"And we'll do better next time, you'll see," she told him with newfound conviction.

Jack tossed his head as though in agreement and heaved a contented sigh. Satisfied that he was happy, Libby left him to finish his feed and walked eagerly toward the comforts of the cottage, her whole body suddenly aching with weariness.

She slept that night in a heavy, dreamless slumber, stirring only once to feel the hard shiny object beneath her pillow. And when she finally woke to see sunshine streaming in through her window she remembered yesterday as if it was a dream. It seemed crazy today to think that someone had taken Jack out in the night. Thank heaven she hadn't gotten around to telling Amy... But what about his performance; what about his lethargic efforts around the jumping course?

She pushed the thoughts to the back of her mind and concentrated her attention on next weekend. She could ride over to the show on Sunday, so she didn't need to ask for a lift. Excitement flooded in as she imagined the look on Becky and Carly's faces when the commentator announced that Jack Flash had jumped a clear round. She would show them, just wait and see.

Libby saw Amy again a lot sooner than she expected, for the

42

next morning after she had turned Jack out into the orchard she heard the sound of hooves scrunching on the gravel and looked across to see Poppy and Amy coming down the drive. The little palomino's ears were pricked sharply forward, and at his heels trotted a small white dog.

"Isn't that Mick, from Broad Oak?" called Libby in surprise. "Or do you have his double?"

Amy grinned, her cheeks bright pink from the fresh clear air, and then she jumped to the ground and pulled off her riding hat, shaking out her cap of tight dark curls.

"That's better," she exclaimed, glancing down at the little dog that was busily sniffing in the bushes. "He just appeared behind me a few minutes ago. I can take him back on my way home, I suppose, but do you think they'll be worrying about him?"

Libby crouched down to scratch the backs of the cute little Highland terrier's ears.

"Worry about Mick?" she exclaimed. "No… I mean they all think the world of him, but he does his own thing. He's very independent, aren't you boy?"

His response was to plant a wet kiss on Libby's face before disappearing up the pathway towards the orchard.

"You don't mind me just turning up like this, do you?" asked Amy, looking suddenly uncomfortable. "I didn't realize that you lived here until I saw your car in the drive, and I thought I'd just… you know… pop in and say hello."

"I'm glad you did," responded Libby. "Jack is turned out in the orchard, so why don't you put Poppy into his stable and come inside for a drink? You look as if you could use one."

"Thanks."

Amy pulled the reins over her pony's tiny dark tipped ears and followed Libby along the orchard gate side of the cottage, waiting until she had taken hold of Jack's head collar before opening the gate.

"You go on ahead," urged Libby. "The stable is just through that gate and up the path. I'll keep hold of Jack until you've left the orchard just in case he upsets Poppy; then I'll catch up."

Jack ran around in a circle, excited by the new arrival, and it was all Libby could do to keep him under control, so it wasn't until Poppy and Amy had disappeared from view that she dared to let him go. He galloped off, bucking wildly, and she watched him for a moment before opening the creaky gate to walk up the path toward the stable. Just ahead of her she could see the little palomino's golden cream rump. He was standing in the pathway, right in the same spot that Jack had refused to pass when he first came to his new home.

"That's funny," she called out. "Jack doesn't like coming along that bit, either. I mean he's all right now, but he still hesitates and snorts. My gran says it has something to do with the holly stump."

When Amy gave her a puzzled look she pointed to the jagged tree stump at the side of the path.

"My dad cut it down," she explained. "and some of the other holly trees in the gardens… Gran thinks it's unlucky or something."

Amy grinned and gave Poppy a whack.

"Well I'm not superstitious," she declared.

The little palomino's huge dark eyes were small slits as he leaped forward, snorting at some invisible monster and cantering sideways, almost knocking Amy over, but Libby followed more slowly, fighting back the sound that filled her head. The sound of the stricken tree... That horrible crack and then the mournful rustling as its shiny, vibrant leaves had settled into an eerie silence.

With a shudder she ran to catch up to Amy, and just as they reached the yard in front of the stable a small white shape came hurtling past.

"Mick," called Libby.

He totally ignored her and ran over toward the stable, peering cautiously through the open door with a growl rumbling in his throat.

"Come here," she cried, catching up behind him, but he evaded her grasp, dashed inside the shadowy interior and made for the furthest corner beneath the hayrack. When Libby followed him inside the hackles on his back were standing on end, and he was growling and barking furiously at an invisible foe.

"There's nothing there," she told him uneasily and then, as his barks became more and more frantic, she suddenly made a grab for him. He squealed as if in terror, and when her fingers slipped he raced outside again, stumpy tail firmly fixed between his short back legs as he raced off down the pathway.

"What's wrong with him?" asked Amy.

Libby squirmed uneasily.

"I don't know," she replied cautiously, trying to ignore the icy tremor that made her legs feel suddenly shaky.

"Well, I suppose I'd better follow him and make sure he gets home all right," said Amy with a sigh. "Let's have that drink another time, OK?"

45

"Definitely," agreed Libby, and as she walked slowly back down the pathway behind Poppy's shiny golden rump she found herself wishing that Amy could stay long enough for her to at least try to share some of her misgivings about the happenings at Holly Bank.

"He must have seen a rat," declared Amy as she mounted up and turned Poppy toward the road.

"I hope so," agreed Libby. "At least… I mean… I don't like rats, but at least then we'd know what might have given him such a terrible fright."

"Well, what else could it have been?" remarked Amy with a frown, and Libby gave a forced laugh.

"Nothing, of course," she said.

Chapter 5

The yard at Broad Oak seemed strangely deserted as Libby led Jack in through the gate. The golden brown chickens were relaxing in a patch of sunlight; feathers plumped out and yellow eyes half closed, while Roger, the speckled gray rooster, stood watch, but they were the only sign of life on the yard, and she suddenly had the weirdest feeling that something was wrong.

Hurriedly she led Jack toward a spare stall and, as she slipped his bridle over his ears, she heard Mary Hunter's deep voice, booming out across the silent yard.

"Libby … Libby."

Jack let the bit go with a clinking sound and Libby turned toward the stable door.

"I'm in here."

The stable owner's broad shape materialized in the square of light above the half door.

"Oh, there you are," she cried, her face crinkling into a thousand tiny lines as she screwed it up into a smile.

Libby gave Jack a final pat and walked toward her.

47

"What's up?" she asked, lifting his saddle onto her hip. Mary opened the door to let her out then carefully bolted it again, and as she turned back to face her Libby noticed that her cool gray eyes were dark with emotion. They darted back and forth as though unable to settle on any one thing, and the forced smile had disappeared to be replaced by a worried frown. Impulsively Libby placed a hand on her arm.

"Is everything OK?"

Mary shook her head slowly.

"I'm afraid not, and I really do need you to do me a favor. It's Mick, you see... he's really distressed and he can't keep anything down. I have a horrible feeling that he swallowed some poison, and I must get him to the vet right away."

Libby's heart lurched; everyone thought the world of Mick, and it was awful to think of him suffering.

"Just tell me what you want me to do," she cried.

"Well, I've got someone coming to see the gray hunter any minute, Jenny's gone out for a ride, and..."

"... And you'd like me to keep them occupied until you get back," finished Libby.

Mary's face crumpled into a grateful smile.

"If you would... All you need to do is let them have a look at him. I shouldn't be long and Marcus will be back any time now; he biked over to see a friend on the other side of the village."

Libby's heart went out to the little dog as Mary placed him carefully into the back of the car, for his normally button bright brown eyes were dull and he was panting heavily, his tongue lolling unnaturally from the side of his mouth. Tears

48

pricked the backs of her eyes as she ran her hand over his soft, white, furry coat.

"He'll be all right," she said firmly but when her eyes met Mary's she knew that they reflected the older woman's fear.

"Hurry up," she whispered as the car engine roared into life, and when it skidded off across the yard she found herself wondering if she would ever see the little dog alive again.

She busied herself by brushing the gray hunter, Duke, swinging the body brush around in rhythmic circles to slide over his coat again and again. One… two… three… then the rasp of the currycomb against the bristles.

"You must be the girl who lives in the haunted house."

The voice behind her made her stop in full flight, brush held aloft as the blood rushed to her face.

"It *is* haunted, isn't it? Haven't you seen any ghosts yet?"

She knew who it was of course, by the arrogant lilt in his voice, even before she turned around to see the mocking laughter in his hazel eyes. His tall lean figure was silhouetted in the open doorway, legs astride, arms folded across his chest and clean cut features stretched into a broad grin.

"What are you talking about?" she asked curtly.

"Holly Bank Cottage," he went on. "I heard it was haunted."

"Well you heard wrong," snapped Libby. "I live there, I should know… anyway… I don't believe in ghosts."

"Well, we have something in common, then," remarked Marcus Hunter. "Anyway, I don't suppose you know where the old girl is, do you?"

"If you mean your mother, Mick has been poisoned and she's taken him to the vet. He's in bad shape."

Libby's heart sank when she saw the expression on

49

Marcus's face. She would have given anything to be able to rephrase her tactlessly chosen words, but it was too late to soften the blow now.

The color drained from his lightly tanned skin, the strong set of his jaw softened as his head fell forward, and her nails dug into the balls of her thumbs as she watched his attractive features crumple.

"He isn't dead."

She blurted out the words, and then stood helplessly as he looked up at her, his eyes dark with emotion.

"… Yet," he yelled. "Why don't you just come out and say he isn't dead… yet?"

Her response came out with a confidence she was far from feeling.

"Because he's gone to the vet and there's every chance that he'll be fine."

"Do you really think so?"

Again his expression changed as hope came flooding back and Libby softened toward the arrogant young man she had already decided to dislike, even before she met him.

"Yes," she said firmly. "If he has been poisoned they'll soon find the antidote, I'm sure of it."

"He's my dog, you know. Christmas present a couple of years ago. The place wouldn't be the same without him."

"Well, it isn't going to be without him," Libby insisted. "Now why don't you go and call the vet before the people arrive to see Duke?"

"Oh no, I'd forgotten about that," groaned Marcus.

"Well hurry up, then," advised Libby.

A dark blue car rolled into the yard as he disappeared in

50

the direction of the cottage. It purred to a halt beside the barn and a tall, gray-haired gentleman climbed out and straightened his tweed jacket, before closing the car door gently and turning toward Libby with a gracious smile.

"Hello! The name's William Richmond, and I'm looking for Mrs. Hunter."

His voice boomed across the stable yard and she smiled back self-consciously.

"If you're here to see the gray hunter I can show you where he is, if you like. Mrs. Hunter will be back soon… and so will her son."

The man nodded enthusiastically.

"Ah, yes, of course, Marcus must be home for summer vacation, I suppose. Nice boy, isn't he? I'll bet he gives you young girls a thrill."

Libby grimaced as an all too familiar surge of irritation made the hairs on the back of her neck prickle.

"Well, he's here now – look," she announced, as Marcus's tall spare figure appeared from around the back of the cottage. "So I'll just leave you two to talk."

Marcus strode toward them with long unhurried strides and patted William Richmond enthusiastically on the back.

"So the master of Faversham foxhounds needs a new hunter, does he? Well, I think we have just the thing."

He looked at Libby pleadingly, and with a heavy sigh she picked up a head collar and went toward Duke's stable.

"Oh, and by the way," he told her as she walked by. "You were right. Mick's got to stay at the vet's for a day or two, but he's going to be fine."

Reluctantly she glanced up and when her eyes caught the

51

mischievous glint in his he winked slowly and she felt a strange, unexpected flutter from somewhere deep inside. It would take more than that for Marcus-precious-Hunter to get into her good graces, she decided, a frown clouding her features.

Marcus just laughed and turned away.

"Right then, William," he began as she slipped the bolt on Duke's door. "Now this is what you call a hunter."

Before they had even gotten around to tacking up the big gray Mary Hunter returned, and as soon as she had parked the car she hurried across toward them.

"Sorry I'm late…" she began but William Richmond would hear none of it.

"Just glad to hear that the little dog is going to be all right," he told her. "And I've been well looked after by Marcus here."

"Not just me," butted in Marcus, but Libby was already walking away.

"Well, what are we waiting for?" asked Mary. "Let's get this horse tacked up."

Steam from the muckheap rose into the fresh clear air as she lifted the handles on her wheelbarrow and heaved them upwards to empty its load, but before she had time to fork it back the sound of another set of hooves heralded Jenny's return. Libby leaned her empty barrow against the wall, deposited her fork on its rack and hurried across to where Jenny's big dark brown Thoroughbred mount had halted impatiently outside the tack room. He sidestepped as his rider slipped to the ground, tossing his head and snorting at an imaginary foe, but Jenny just shook her head at his antics and handed his reins to Libby.

"Here you are," she said with a smile. "I've had enough of him for one day. No wonder Emma gets me to exercise him for her. He's a total liability on the road."

Libby patted his gleaming bronze neck.

"But good at cross country," she remarked.

"The best," agreed Jenny. "And if you'll see to him for me I'll give you that jumping lesson I promised."

A broad, excited grin was all the reply she needed.

Libby felt totally focused by the time she had seen to the fractious Thoroughbred, and she tacked Jack up and headed for the outdoor ring with a new sense of purpose. Never mind Marcus Hunter and his comments, this was what it was all about: she and Jack Flash would prove themselves to everyone at the horse show this weekend.

"You and me," she told the powerful bay gelding, and he nodded his head as if in agreement and broke into a prancing trot.

Amy arrived while they were still working. She leaned on the fence to watch, willing her newfound friend to do well, and Libby gave her a wave as she passed by in a working trot.

"We'll go out for a ride after my lesson, if you want," she called.

Amy nodded enthusiastically.

"Concentrate, Libby," ordered Jenny. "And get him more around your inside leg, that's it. Now you can come to the trotting poles, but keep him straight and don't lose your rhythm."

Jenny wouldn't allow Libby to let Jack out of trot until he was totally obedient, and then the canter had to be perfect. By the time the grid had been built up from three simple poles to a bounce followed by an upright to a spread, Libby's muscles were beginning to ache.

"Keep your legs on," yelled Jenny. "You can't expect him to jump if you're not there."

Elation flooded over her as Jack tucked right up and ballooned over the last parallel, and she allowed him to canter around the ring on a loose rein before slowing to a walk.

Jenny's face was beaming.

"He really is going to be something special," she remarked. "As long as you keep up with the ground work and don't let him get too stupid. Patience, that's the key."

"Patience," repeated Libby, still floating on a euphoric cloud.

Amy had hooked Poppy's reins around her arm and allowed him to graze while she watched Libby's progress, and now she gathered them up, led him into the ring and clambered into the saddle.

"My turn, Jenny," she called, urging the little pony into canter. "We'll show you how it's done."

She headed Poppy towards a cross pole with a broad grin on her face and when (as usual) he dug in his toes and stopped dead in front of it, she just sat up, pulled a comical face and shrugged.

"Oh, well," she exclaimed. "Maybe not today."

Libby and Jenny doubled up with laughter as the little palomino stared in horror at the red and white fence.

"Perhaps show jumping isn't quite your thing," suggested

Jenny, biting her bottom lip. Amy just giggled and threw her arms around Poppy's neck.

"I don't think we have a '*thing*,'" she groaned.

"Oh, yes you do."

Jenny walked toward her and ran her hand over his glistening golden coat.

"He has lovely conformation, and he's a true stamp of a Welsh Mountain pony. You could show him in hand."

"Of course," cried Libby. "In mountain and moorland classes."

"I'll give you a hand tomorrow afternoon, if you like," Jenny told her. "You know, show you how to lead him properly."

Amy's face glowed with excitement.

"I'll help you muck out every day if you do," she promised.

"I'll hold you to that," smiled Jenny.

The rest of the day passed in a haze of excitement. Amy could think of little else but the show. For the very first time she was actually going to take part and, holding her own hopes and fears close against her chest, Libby listened to her friend's high pitched chatter and willed her to do well, imagining the look on Carly and Becky's faces if she and Amy both won a prize.

It wasn't until she rode slowly home that evening that her thoughts strayed back again to Marcus Hunter. He was exactly as she had expected him to be; totally arrogant and so full of himself that she couldn't understand why everyone kept singing his praises. Look how he'd tried to frighten her with his comments about her living in a haunted house. To make something like that up just to try and scare her was down-right mean. If it was just made up, said an inner voice, but she discounted it instantly. And when a fleeting image of his face, dark with misery after her blunt delivery of the information about poor Mick, flicked into her mind, she pushed it firmly away and turned her thoughts once again to her dreams. She and Jack would show them all this weekend, she was sure of it.

When her heart began to thud in her chest and a prickle of excitement bubbled up at the base of her throat, she urged her eager mount into trot, trying to take her mind away from the nerves that made her stomach churn.

"Think positive," she told herself, taking a big deep breath. "We can do it... can't we, boy?"

The following week passed by so quickly that Libby hardly had time to dwell on her fears about Jack, but the key to his stable remained beneath her pillow, just in case. Sometimes, in the dead of night, she would wake and feel for its cold smooth hardness, and then fall asleep again to hear the echo of hooves in her dreams. But every morning he was there, waiting for her, his eyes bright and shining with eagerness for the day ahead, and gradually her fears began to fade away completely. All she and Amy could think about was the show, and as she rode home the night before, having given Jack a complete bath at Broad Oak before she left, Libby couldn't decide if she was longing for tomorrow or dreading it.

"A bit of both, eh boy?" she admitted as she dismounted outside the back door of Holly Bank.

Her grandmother was waiting impatiently.

"Come on, honey," she urged from the open doorway. "Your supper is ready. Go and put Jack away and I'll help you to clean your tack."

"Thanks Gran," smiled Libby. "What would I do without you?"

When the big bay gelding was settled for the night with a clean bed of snow-white shavings and a full share of sweet smelling hay, Libby locked the stable door carefully, watching with satisfaction as the silver key clicked home, securing her precious horse.

"Sleep tight," she murmured, but he just chewed contentedly, totally ignoring her, and she walked back toward the cottage with a warm feeling deep inside. Everything was all right, she was sure of it.

Chapter 6

When Libby arrived at the crossroads the next morning Amy was already there, her bright face pink with half-hidden excitement. Poppy's silver mane glistened in the early morning sunshine and his carefully shampooed coat took on the hue of pure gold.

"He looks great," cried Libby. "You're sure to win."

"If only," responded Amy with a wry smile. "Anyway, Jack looks pretty darned good."

"Yes, but looks don't matter in my class."

"Unless you go in the best turned out," suggested Amy.

Libby grinned.

"Maybe I will," she said.

They fell in together then, side-by-side, Jack walking as slowly as Libby could persuade him to while Poppy kept trotting to catch up. Both girls fell silent, their heads far too full of what the day might bring for idle conversation. The sun was shining and the horses beneath them were bursting with energy. Today anything was possible.

When an array of brightly painted horse trailers came into view, drawn up in neat lines in a field just ahead, Libby felt her stomach gurgle and she glanced across at Amy to see if her nerves echoed in her friend's face.

"Something's fluttering in my stomach," she groaned.

Amy gave a pasty grin.

"Never mind butterflies. I seem to have a flock of crows in mine," she giggled.

The jumping course was already set out, gaudily bright against the green of the newly mown grass. All around were horses – bays, grays and chestnuts – trotting around in endless circles.

"There are Becky and Carly," cried Amy, waving, but as Murphy and Tango cantered toward them she pulled a face.

"If they start making jokes about Poppy I'll…"

Libby cut her off in mid-sentence.

"Don't mind what they say. Just show them that they're wrong," she said, lowering her voice as Tango skidded to a halt beside them.

Carly's huge eyes were feverishly bright and two bright spots of color marked her cheeks.

"Marcus is here," she announced, her voice tight with excitement. "He's brought those two new youngsters that arrived the other day. He's taking them in the novice jumping."

Libby's heart sank.

"So he'll be in my class," groaned Libby, wondering why it bothered her so much.

"Maybe you'll beat him," remarked Amy.

Becky let out an amused shriek.

"As if," she giggled, heading Murphy off toward the collecting ring. He arched his neck and chomped on his bit, obedient as always, and Amy sighed.

"Isn't he just the most beautiful horse?" she said.

"Nicer than Poppy?" asked Libby, and Amy's face fell.

"Of course not," she cried, jumping to her pony's defense. "Just… you know… different."

When Amy had disappeared in the direction of ring three to get ready for her mountain and moorland class, Libby waited nervously beside the jumping ring watching the other competitors in her class practicing. She was twelfth to go, so she didn't want to tire Jack out by overdoing it. After the next two I'll go over the practice fence, she told herself, concentrating hard on the course to try and get control of the nerves that were turning her insides into a bubbling mess.

At first she didn't hear the loud voice from just behind her, so its owner yelled loudly in her ear, and she looked around with a start to see Marcus Hunter sitting astride a big gelding.

"Well, if it isn't the girl from the haunted house again," he remarked with a grin.

"I told you… I don't believe in ghosts," declared Libby as she felt her face turn embarrassingly pink. "Anyway, what do you know about Holly Bank?"

He shrugged, turning his attention to where a small bay had just stopped at the triple bar for the third time.

"Nothing really, just that it is supposed to be haunted. Anyway, it seems to be my turn. Wish me luck."

Libby watched in envy as he cantered off toward the practice fence, jumped it with ease and carried straight on into the ring with the kind of calm confidence she longed for. The bay and white gelding spooked once or twice and tried to stop at the brush fence, but with quiet determination Marcus rode it positively forward, and when it ballooned over the last parallel he never even moved in the saddle. Becky and Carly were right about one thing, thought Libby. He certainly could ride. It gave her goose bumps just to watch him.

She felt oddly pleased when he walked the skewbald out of the ring on a long rein and rode straight toward her, patting its neck enthusiastically.

"Did well for his first attempt, didn't he?" he asked, looking up. "Anyway, I'd better go and get the gray. Good luck."

He smiled then. A genuine friendly smile, and Libby felt her hostility towards him beginning to fade.

"I'll need it," she laughed, pushing Jack into trot.

Inspired by Marcus's performance Libby cantered determinedly toward the practice fence, and when the horse beneath her leaped over it in a huge explosive bound she felt her confidence soar.

"Number twenty six," called a voice from the ringside as she jumped it for the second time, and she headed for the entrance, her legs firmly clasped around Jack's sides and her heart beating so loudly that it seemed to reverberate around inside her head. The loud jarring sound of the bell, however, jerked her into action, and as soon as she headed for the first fence in a powerful, rhythmic canter, her nerves disappeared and adrenalin took over.

The first fences seemed to come just right, until they came to the dreaded red wall. Libby over-checked, Jack hesitated, and for a moment she thought he was going to put in an impossibly short stride. Inside her head she heard Jenny's voice.

"Use your legs… Kick him on."

She dug in her heels and he lifted beneath her, a good half stride too far off. And then they were flying through the air, way above the looming obstacle, and galloping on to the next.

After that there was no way that Jack was going to touch anything, and as they cantered through the finishing posts Libby threw her arms around his neck.

"Well, there is an enthusiastic young lady," called the commentator. "Clear round for Libby Blackstock and Jack Flash."

For Libby it was like a dream come true. She didn't care what happened in the jump off; she had her clear round and Jack had jumped like the star she knew he was.

"Well done," called a familiar voice and she saw Jenny Harris's small, straight-backed figure, standing by the practice fence."

"You *did* yell at me to kick on," cried Libby. "I thought it was my imagination."

Jenny laughed.

"Glad you heard me," she said. "I'm just altering the practice fence for Marcus. Are you going in the jump off?"

Libby gave her a puzzled frown.

"Of course I am."

"Well, don't go too fast," advised Jenny. "Not if you want him to be really good, that is. You'd be surprised how many horses are ruined by being chased against the clock before they're ready. It does their heads in."

"Thanks," responded Libby as her dream of a red rosette faded.

"Try and make some tight turns if you can," continued Jenny. "And push on a bit, but don't lose your rhythm. That way you can save time without turning your horse into a lunatic."

"I'll do that," smiled Libby.

She ended up by being a very creditable third behind Marcus with the gray, as the horses that really galloped all knocked fences down, and Jack jumped another good clear round.

"Well done," Marcus told her as they stood in line to receive their rosettes, and her heart glowed with pride.

"Well done yourself," she replied.

All in all it was the kind of day that dreams are made of, especially when Poppy came back with a red rosette, and the two girls could talk of nothing else as they prepared to ride home. All her memories of Jack's last performance, when she thought he had been ridden in the night, seemed a million miles away, and Libby decided to share her secret with Amy on the way home; then they could have a good laugh about it and she could put her fears firmly behind her once and for all.

She broached the subject as they turned into the lane that led to Broad Oak. Both horses were walking quietly, blowing gently with their efforts of the day, while their riders fell silent, basking in a mellow glow of happiness.

"Did you know that Holly Bank was supposed to be haunted?"

Libby's question came right out of the blue, and for a moment Amy just looked at her with a vaguely puzzled expression.

"It's probably just an old wives' tale," she said in a matter of fact tone. "Why… you don't believe in ghosts, do you?"

Libby looked at the horizon.

"Of course not," she said too quickly. "I just… you know… wondered if you knew anything about it."

Amy leaned down and patted Poppy's shoulder, and then reached forward to straighten the red rosette that still fluttered from his brow band.

"Why… you haven't seen anything, have you?" she giggled. "You know… things that go bump in the night… or white figures floating about."

"Don't be silly."

Libby's response was sharper than she intended, and a troubled frown replaced the happy expression on Amy's face.

"It really does bother you, doesn't it? The idea of Holly Bank being haunted."

Libby shook her head and gathered up her reins.

"No… not really. It's just…"

"Just what?" Amy's dark eyes glinted with determination. "Tell me what *is* bothering you."

Libby sighed, a deep, long held sigh of relief.

"Just that there are so many things lately that don't add up."

"Like what?" demanded Amy.

"Like the way Mick behaved in the stable, and the fact that both Jack and Poppy are spooky about going up the path past the holly stump."

"But that could be anything," laughed Amy.

"And the fact that I think someone took Jack out in the night and rode him into the ground," she blurted out.

Amy stared at her then in shocked silence, and Libby went

on to tell her friend, in a calm deliberate tone, everything that happened on the morning of the show … the morning she had found Jack covered in sweat stains and mud. She had almost managed to convince herself that it had all been in her imagination until this moment, but as she relayed all the details to Amy and remembered just how exhausted he had been, the awful fear came creeping back and she knew she had been kidding herself.

"And you think that what happened to Jack is linked to the cottage being haunted," gasped Amy.

Libby stared at her wide-eyed.

"Oh… no… At least I don't think so. I don't want to think so."

She felt a shiver creeping up her spine as a fleeting image flashed into her mind, of a shadowy figure in the light of the moon; now that really must have been her imagination playing tricks.

"Of course not," she went on determinedly. "Obviously it was just kids or something. Anyway, I've got a good padlock on the stable door now, so I don't need to worry anymore."

Amy narrowed her eyes, recognizing the forced lightness in her friend's tone.

"And what did your grandmother say about it?" she asked.

Libby shrugged and urged Jack forward.

"I didn't want to worry her," she admitted. "Or of course it might have been Becky and Carly's idea of a joke."

"Not their style," commented Amy, shaking her head.

They rode in silence, their euphoric mood strangely dampened, until Amy suddenly started to giggle.

"You should have seen your face when I suggested that

Jack's midnight ride might have something to do with Holly Bank being haunted," she shrieked. "You looked as if you really had seen a ghost."

"Well, what do you expect?" blurted out Libby.

"Sorry," muttered Amy. "But Mick could have been barking at anything, and you don't really *believe* in ghosts, do you? Surely you could have been mistaken about Jack?"

"I've thought and thought about that," admitted Libby. "Sometimes I think I imagined it, but then now, telling you, it all seemed kind of real again."

"Well if anything like it happens again you can pick up the phone and call me," Amy told her. "And I'm sure that if anyone really did ride Jack, well, it must just have been someone joking around. Maybe it was the Baker twins; they're always pulling stunts."

Libby had seen the two mischievous twelve-year-olds from the village hanging around in the lane on more than one occasion, and she suddenly felt as if a weight had been lifted from her shoulders.

"Of course," she cried, "that makes sense. And they can ride; I've seen them out on that old Thoroughbred of Mr. Myers."

"There you are," said Amy. "If we see them around again we'll ask them about it. But if does make sense. I can't believe you didn't tell anyone, though."

Libby started to giggle. "Actually, I did," She admitted. "When Jack jumped that awful round at the last show and he felt so tired, I told Becky and Carly that I thought someone had ridden him in the night."

"I can imagine their reaction to that, " hooted Amy.

"Exactly," smiled Libby. "They thought I was making up excuses."

"Well, you certainly didn't need any excuses today."

Libby smiled at her new friend and everything seemed to slip into place.

"And neither did you," she told her.

Amy reached forward to touch the red rosette, her face glowing with pride.

"Come on," she urged. "I can't wait to show this to my dad," then a shadow clouded her features. "I only wish I could show it to my mom," she sighed.

"Well, I can't show mine to either of my parents," declared Libby in an effort to cheer her up.

"But at least you know that your mother is coming back one day," responded Amy, and Libby felt emotion choke her throat. It must be so bad to lose a parent.

"It must have been awful for you," she murmured, feeling suddenly awkward. What did you say to someone whose mother had been killed?

"Maybe your dad will find someone else," she eventually suggested. "Then at least you'll have a proper family again."

"He's already found someone," snapped Amy. Suddenly remembering Carly's dad's comments on the journey home from the show, Libby felt a wave of guilt.

"Don't you get along with her?" she asked, desperate to get back onto comfortable ground but unsure of what to say.

"No one can take my mother's place," declared Amy, and the violence in her tone made Libby feel uneasy. Maybe she should encourage her to talk about it.

"Maybe you'll learn to like her eventually," she suggested brightly. "I mean, I know she'll never be your mother, but…"

"… Perhaps I could give her a chance?" finished Amy. "That's what my dad is always saying. *'Margaret cares about you, Margaret worries about you. Margaret really wants to get along with you.'*"

"Well, maybe she does," remarked Libby.

"But all she ever does is nag at me," insisted Amy and Libby smiled.

"Sometimes I feel as if that's all my mother ever does," she admitted.

"Honestly?" cried Amy.

"Honestly," said Libby. "But I know that it's only because she cares about me."

As Amy said goodbye Libby noticed a thoughtful expression on her face, and she smiled to herself. Perhaps their conversation really had made her friend stop and think. Oh, she hoped so.

Chapter 7

When Libby came bursting into the kitchen, Mollie Blackstock looked around from where she was peeling carrots at the sink.

"Your mother called earlier," she remarked. "She said to give you her love."

"Darn!" groaned Libby. "I always seem to miss her."

Mollie smiled and shook her neat, white-haired head.

"That, my dear, is because you spend your life dashing about."

For a moment Libby stopped and looked at her grandmother, and then she reached across and took hold of her arm.

"I'm neglecting you, aren't I?" she asked, feeling suddenly guilty as she realized just how little time she seemed to have spent at home in the weeks since her parents went away, but Mollie just laughed.

"Oh don't you worry about me," she insisted. "I have plenty to fill my days. I've made a new friend at the pensioners club in the village. His name is Harry Redman, and he's lived around here all his life."

Libby stopped in her tracks, eyes like saucers.

"Gran!" she exclaimed.

Mollie laughed, her face pink with delight.

"I am allowed to have a gentleman friend you know," she said. "Anyway, go and get yourself changed. Supper is ready, and you can tidy that disgusting room of yours this evening."

Libby groaned.

"But there's a really good show on TV, and..." she began.

"Well, you'd better hurry up, hadn't you?" insisted Mollie sternly.

Libby smiled affectionately as her grandmother attempted a fierce expression; then she ran across and gave her a quick hug.

"And I thought I was going to have an easy time with you," she laughed. "Why, you're even more bossy than Mom!"

Mollie's eyes twinkled.

"Well that's good; someone has to keep you in order after all. Oh, and by the way, make sure you're home for supper at a reasonable time day after tomorrow."

A warm flush of color flooded her pale complexion as she spoke, and Libby looked at her thoughtfully for a moment before letting out a loud hoot.

"He's coming, isn't he... this Harry person? He's coming for dinner."

"His name," announced Mollie. "Is Harry Redman, Mr. Redman to you, and he is just a friend. I want you to meet him, that's all."

"Don't worry, Gran," promised Libby. "I won't let you down, you'll see, and I'm going to clean my room right now."

She arrived late at Broad Oak the next morning and the first person she saw was Amy, busily filling water buckets at the tap in the yard.

"I thought I'd start, as I intend to keep going with Jenny," Amy called, shutting off the water and heaving the buckets off the ground.

"Jenny said she'd give Poppy and me some lessons if I helped out," she explained.

"Great," agreed Libby, taking one of the buckets from her. "There is another club show on the twenty-eighth of next month, and I think it's a qualifier for the championships at the end of the season. Poppy would have a good chance."

Amy grimaced.

"Jenny says he needs to learn to stand up better, and I have to teach him to be more obedient when I lead him."

"Jenny just tries to make us work harder," smiled Libby. "She says that the difference between true professionals and amateurs is that amateurs practice until they get it right and professionals practice until they can't get it wrong."

"Hmm," remarked Amy with a slight frown. "I'll have to think about that one. Come on, you can help me finish Flipper's stall. It's the last one."

When they rounded the corner of the barn, still chattering about Jenny's wise statement, they heard a loud yapping and a bundle of white fluff came charging toward them from the direction of the cottage.

"Mick!" cried Libby, dumping her bucket on the floor and reaching out her arms towards the little dog. "You are better…"

A face appeared from over the half door of a stall just beside them.

71

"He certainly is," announced Marcus Hunter, his grin stretching from ear to ear.

"It'll take more than a bit of rat poison to get the better of Micky boy… won't it, boy?"

The little dog looked up at him, button bright eyes shining and stumpy tail wagging furiously.

"Well, we're really glad he's better," declared Amy while Libby, suddenly speechless, just nodded in agreement.

Marcus gave the big chestnut he was grooming an affectionate slap and came out onto the yard, flipping the kick bolt behind him.

"I'm taking Moses here out for some exercise after lunch," he told them. "Why don't you two come with me? We could take the bridle path that goes over the field."

Libby stood with her mouth open, feeling stupid, but Amy laughed, her dark eyes sparkling with excitement.

"Well, if you don't mind pitting yourself against Poppy," she agreed. "Although of course you two will never catch me with your clumsy big horses."

Marcus grinned.

"That's what you think," he told her. "Anyway…"

He looked straight at Libby, eyes narrowed, hiding his expression.

"What about your Jack? He can certainly jump, but can he gallop?"

Libby returned his gaze, jutting out her chin, and when an unexpected lurching sensation forced the air from her lungs she lowered her gaze to catch her breath.

"Well, you'll just have to wait and see, won't you?" she told him, turning away.

The two girls sat on the seat by the tack room to eat their lunch. They were both strangely quiet. Even Amy, who insisted that Marcus Hunter definitely did not impress her, chewed thoughtfully.

"Of course Poppy won't really beat you both," she suddenly announced.

"It would be a miracle if he did with those little short legs," agreed Libby.

"Imagine Marcus's face if he did," remarked Amy and both girls began to giggle, leaning forward to clutch their stomachs in laughter at the vision of the tiny, golden pony, streaking ahead of his two huge, powerful companions.

"Can anyone join in?" called Carly as she approached from the direction of the paddock, swinging a head collar to and fro. Her sandy hair blew gently behind her in the breeze, and her long slim legs were encased in ink-blue, suede-seated jodhpurs. Libby felt a prickle of envy and her laughter died.

"We were just talking about our ride this afternoon," she said.

Carly frowned.

"With Marcus!" blurted out Amy. "He's asked us to go for a trail ride after lunch."

Unused to Amy's impulsive tongue, Libby could have happily throttled her, and when Carly's face lit up her heart sank.

"That's it!" Libby moaned as the ink-blue jodhpurs disappeared in the direction of the barn. "You do realize that we'll now have the company of those two."

Amy's face fell.

"Me and my big mouth," she groaned, but Libby shrugged.

"Never mind," she giggled. "Maybe Poppy will out-gallop Murphy, and maybe Tango as well."

The ride turned out to be more fun than any of them could have imagined, even though, as Libby had predicted, Carly and Becky appeared – immaculately turned out, of course – as soon as they set off. Marcus, however, didn't seem to mind their tagging along, and in fact he surprised everyone with his madcap humor and sense of fun.

All in all, decided Libby as she rode slowly homeward, it had been a nearly perfect day, even if Poppy hadn't won the crazy race across the field.

She smiled to herself as she remembered how valiantly the little palomino pony had tried to keep up. Why, even Becky had made some pleasant remarks about him. Perhaps she and Carly weren't so bad after all, and Marcus – she closed her eyes dreamily. Marcus was definitely a whole lot nicer than she had given him credit for.

The glow stayed with her as she took care of Jack, carefully padlocking his door, of course, but smiling to herself as she did so. Her fears for him suddenly seemed distant and unrealistic. She held the shiny silver key out in front of her before slipping it into her pocket. Did Amy think she was crazy, she wondered, or was her new friend just humoring her by listening to her wild ideas and trying to help? She imagined the bright, honest expression in Amy's eyes and smiled to herself. No, she realized, one thing she had found out about her friend was that, no matter what, she always spoke her mind.

The events of the day filled Libby's dreams that night. Poppy galloping over the field, his rider's face glowing with delight as her tiny mount surged past Marcus's powerful chestnut, and dear Jack Flash, pounding beneath her, muscles taut with effort… And then she half-woke in wonder to see her room filled with an eerie silver glow. She blinked, torn between dreams and reality as wild shadows raced across the ceiling, but sleep closed over her again, drawing her back into its comforting folds so that even when the distant sound of galloping hooves penetrated her subconscious, she couldn't claw her way out of the shadows.

Libby walked slowly up the pathway toward Jack's stable. She was going to be late to Broad Oak, but she knew that Mary Hunter and Jenny didn't expect her to go in early every day, so she took her time breathing in the fresh morning air and going over the events of yesterday as she approached the pathway that led past the holly stump.

She didn't notice the silence until she was nearly there, didn't feel how cold the air had become, didn't realize that Jack was not looking impatiently over his door until she fumbled in her pocket for the silver key. And then she heard a sound, a heavy rhythmic sound… Someone was breathing right behind her. She spun around as silence fell again. There was nothing there, nothing but the soft green of the trees… and the ugly sawed-off holly stump.

"Pull yourself together, Libby," she told herself sharply, and with another quick glance behind her, she stepped forward and peered over the half door into Jack's stable.

The big bay gelding was standing at the very back of his stall… just as before. His head was down, his nostrils flared at her, deep red against the black of his muzzle, and his silky coat was dark with sweat. Libby stood stock still for a moment fighting for breath; her limbs frozen into immobility as the world came tumbling down around her. And then Jack moved toward her, expecting help, expecting her to take away the pain and confusion that filled his huge, dark eyes.

A wave of anger rushed over Libby, pushing away the initial heart-stopping fear. How dare they? How dare anyone break into her horse's stable…? But they hadn't broken in, had they? The lock shone in the sunshine and she grabbed hold of it, yanking it sharply, expecting it to be broken, and when it defied her efforts she clumsily pushed in the key, turning it with awkward fingers.

It clicked open easily, taking her by surprise, and for a moment she hesitated, unable to believe what was happening. Shaking her head she blinked, and then reality flooded in and she raced across toward her precious horse, her own fear set on hold, because he was all that really mattered.

Once out in the sunshine, tied up to the ring on the wall, to Libby's relief Jack dug into his breakfast with relish while she looked him over. His belly and legs were splattered with mud and his whole body was crusted with dried sweat. There was a piece of bramble tangled into his tail, and one of his shoes was loose. This time there was no question about it. Someone had taken Jack out at night and ridden him hard. But how? How had they gotten him out of his stable without breaking the lock? The obvious answer clicked into place.

They must have had a key. But there was only one key, and that was under her pillow.

Panic flooded in again; she had to tell someone, and someone had to see the state he was in, or no one would ever believe her. But there was only her Gran. She hesitated before racing off toward the cottage, and as she approached the kitchen door she was still unsure. Was it really fair to worry the elderly lady? Perhaps she should be rushing over to see the Baker twins instead.

The decision was taken from her when she saw Mollie's car disappearing down the lane. She stood on the back step, indecisive, unable to concentrate as desperation set in. And then Amy's bright friendly face slipped into her mind. "Any time," she had insisted on the way home from the show when Libby had finally plucked up the courage to share her fears about Jack. "You can call me at any time." Well, the time was now.

Libby's fingers shook as she dialed Amy's number. What should she say?

"Hello, Thomas residence, Margaret speaking."

The voice on the other end of the line sounded brisk and efficient.

"Is Amy there?" stuttered Libby. "Please… I need to talk to Amy."

For just a second there was a heavy silence and then the woman's clipped tones rang in her ears again.

"She hasn't been well, I'm afraid. I told her to stay in bed this morning. Who shall I say called?"

"Just tell her… Libby. Please tell her I need to see her."

The phone clicked down with empty finality and Libby

sank onto a chair with her head in her hands, feeling totally lost and alone.

But then she remembered that Jack was still tied up outside his stall, needing attention, and she knew that fear was a luxury she could ill afford. Slowly she rose to her feet and went out into the fresh morning sunshine, gazing in confusion at the beauty of the day. It seemed so normal and real and just… well… like any other day, and already her mind was turning toward the practicalities. First of all she needed to groom Jack, and then she would get away from here and ride over to Broad Oak. If the worst came to the worst she could always ask Mary Hunter if she could stable him there for a while. And yet, deep down she knew that that would be her very last option. There had to be a reason for this; there had to be a way to sort it out.

When she led Jack past the jagged holly stump half an hour later she refused to acknowledge the icy draft that turned her blood cold. This had nothing to do with ghosts and superstitious nonsense about holly trees, she was sure of it. It had to be those Baker twins; yes, that was it. She would go and see them as soon as she could. How dare they think they could get away with it?

As she moved away the stricken holly tree, wilting in neglected discomfort beside the path, seemed to shiver in a sudden breeze, and beside her she felt Jack's whole body quiver.

Chapter 8

Once at Broad Oak, Libby tried to escape the mind-blowing fear that threatened to suffocate her, by concentrating on any task that would keep her busy. She needed to tell someone so much, but every time she tried to bring up the subject the words just stuck in her throat.

"What's the matter with you this morning?" asked Jenny Harris as she watched Libby sweeping the yard. "You'll wear yourself out if you keep going at that rate."

Libby looked up and forced a smile onto her face.

"And you look as if you've lost your best friend," Jenny went on.. "Why don't you go and take that horse of yours out for a ride... although... come to think of it..."

Her forehead puckered into a puzzled frown.

"He looks almost as miserable as you today."

Libby opened her mouth to speak.

Oh, how she wanted to say those words, but they just wouldn't come out. She couldn't seem to force herself to share her fear. If only Amy were here! Amy would understand... wouldn't she?

By lunchtime she couldn't stand it any longer. She decided she would go home and try to phone her friend again. If Amy was still too ill to come to the phone, then she'd just have to tell her grandmother.

She rode slowly along the lane to Holly Bank, as Jack felt so weary that her heart burst with pity for her usually vibrant, lively horse. Now he walked with head down and flanks heaving, his every step such an effort that eventually she jumped down and walked beside him.

Once back at Holly Bank, she settled him into his stable with feed and a full supply of hay and carefully padlocked his door. How had he gotten out without breaking the lock? Had he jumped over the half door? She eyed it carefully and shook her head. No, impossible; he wouldn't even fit through the gap, and he hardly could have jumped back in again.

She dragged her toes along the pathway, deliberately refusing to look at the holly stump, and when she reached the cottage, with a rush of relief she noticed Mollie's car in the driveway. She would try Amy again right now, and then speak to her grandmother, she decided.

"You're back early," called Mollie as she walked into the kitchen. Libby nodded.

"I felt a bit tired," she mumbled.

Her grandmother frowned.

"Libby Blackstock," she cried. "In all the years I have known you I have never heard you admit to being tired. You must be ill. What is it… the flu… sore throat? Oh, no! And Harry is coming for supper today."

Libby placed a hand on her grandmother's arm.

"I'm fine," she insisted. "I just thought I'd get back and see if you wanted a hand."

Mollie looked at her granddaughter with a cautious expression.

"You want to help me?" she asked in disbelief.

"Yes," insisted Libby. "Just as soon as I've phoned Amy."

The telephone rang and rang in her ears. She put down the receiver with a bang and then picked it up and dialed again, just to be sure she had dialed the right number. It trilled loudly in the silence until a clipped voice came on and told her no one was home. With a sinking heart she left a message and went back into the kitchen.

Mollie Blackstock was leaning over the stove, carefully removing a perfectly baked cake from the oven, while its enticing aroma wafted through the whole house, bringing a kind of very real comfort.

"Gran…" began Libby.

Mollie looked up, her gray eyes bright against the pink of her face.

"I thought I'd make a proper roast," she said. "You know, good old roast beef with roasted potatoes and gravy. Harry could do with a few home comforts; he's been living on his own for the last ten years."

Libby noted the contained excitement in her grandmother's gray eyes and grinned.

"Oh yes," she said. "It's your big date, isn't it?"

"Well I'd hardly call it a big date," she retorted huffily, picking up the delicious smelling cake. "And no sneaking a piece of this when I'm not looking."

Libby picked up the phone in the family room, willing her friend to be in. Amy was the only person who might even try to understand her fears; she knew that now. If only she could contact her.

"Please be there," she whispered, pressing each digit carefully and speaking the number out loud as she did, just to be sure she had it right.

"I'm not home right now, but if you leave your message after the tone…"

When the mechanical voice on the answering machine rang in her ears she banged the receiver down in desperation. Now what was she going to do?

Jack seemed happy now, unaffected by the perils of the night, or so it seemed. He chomped into his hay, chewing rhythmically while Libby watched like an anxious mother. Then she double-checked the padlock and headed for the cottage. She dreaded meeting this Harry Redman person. The last thing she wanted to do was make small talk. Perhaps she should be going over to talk to the Baker twins.

A strange vehicle in the driveway heralded his arrival, and she paused in surprise to look at it. Not quite what one might expect for a friend of Gran's, she thought, running her hand over the gleaming paintwork of the sleek red sports car.

As she peered through the window a deep cough from behind her made her jump, and when she looked around to meet a pair of piercing blue eyes, her face rapidly colored up to match the car.

"Well, do you approve?" called Harry Redman. "Or do

you think your grandmother's friends should drive small, sensible cars like hers?"

"Well... I... I ..." she began, but he simply laughed, a great booming genuine laugh of delight.

"Of course they should," he cried. "But what do I care? I presume you must be Libby, and you have every right to be cautious where your grandmother is concerned."

"I'm not," insisted Libby, and he frowned.

"Well, you should be," he told her. "She is a charming lady with, I might add, an exceptionally charming grand-daughter."

Harry Redman, Libby realized over supper, was quite a character, tall and long-winded with a wild mop of gray hair. He was also surprisingly charming and obviously very taken with Mollie. They giggled like a couple of teenagers throughout the whole meal, and she almost managed to put her ever-present fears on hold for a while; until he brought up the subject of ghosts, that is.

They were just about to start on desert, a creamy concoction of strawberries and meringue, when Harry put down his spoon and grinned mischievously.

"You haven't seen the ghost yet, then?" he asked.

Libby felt a cold shudder run through her body, and she concentrated hard on her plate.

"I've heard something about it," she told him. "But I don't believe in all that superstitious stuff. Why, what do you know about it?"

Harry raised his spoon in the air and waved it around.

"Oh, nothing really, just that this place was once supposed to be haunted by a ruthless highwayman."

"A highwayman!" cried Libby. "You mean a highwayman once lived in this cottage?"

Harry laughed.

"I thought you didn't believe in all that superstitious stuff."

"Well… I don't," declared Libby.

Harry spooned some desert into his mouth and chewed thoughtfully.

"But you would like to know more…" he remarked, his bright blue eyes twinkling mischievously from beneath bushy gray brows.

Libby looked down nervously. Somehow she knew – however much she didn't want it to be – that there was a link between this… highwayman, and her fears about Jack. It seemed ridiculous when she said it out loud, but it was there, all the time it was there, like the beating of her heart.

"I can't remember all the details now but I have a book about it somewhere," Harry continued. "Call on me at my house tomorrow and I'll fill you in on the full story. It's the big square stone house next to the church, right in the center of the village."

Libby's eyes opened wide.

"You mean the one with the horse's heads on the gateposts?"

Harry nodded, his bushy gray hair quivering like a halo around his head.

"That's right. I'll be in all afternoon," then he looked across at Mollie with affection in his eyes. "Bring your gran if you like."

Mollie's face fell.

84

"As much as I'd love to come, its the women's institute annual general meeting tomorrow, and I promised to take cakes."

"Well if they are as good as this desert I wish I were going," remarked Harry.

Libby left them then, happy in each other's company, and went through into the family room, her head filled with Harry Redman's casually given information. A highwayman, here at Holly Bank, seemed ridiculous. And yet didn't her crazy ideas about Jack being ridden in the night seem ridiculous? With shaking finger she dialed Amy's number again, closing her eyes tightly as she listened to the shrill tone on the other end of the line. Begging her to be there.

"I am sorry, but there is no one home right now…"

At the sound of the clipped tones of the voice on the answering machine, she replaced the receiver and placed her head in her hands, desperation flooding her whole body. What was she going to do tonight? How could she leave Jack alone again to face… whatever? There was only one thing to do. She would have to spend the night in the stable with him.

As soon as the thought came into her mind she dismissed it. It was just too scary to even contemplate. But how else could she try to protect her precious horse? He had no one else. And then she knew, with dreaded certainty, that she had no other choice.

Libby kissed her grandmother's soft cheek, breathing in her flowery fragrance, suddenly becoming intensely aware of all the sights and sounds around her as if it were the last time she would ever experience them.

85

"I'm going up," Mollie told her, reaching out a hand to touch her granddaughter's face with gentle fingers. "You will switch out the lights, won't you?"

Libby nodded, clutching at her hand, and for a moment the old lady's brow puckered in concern.

"Are you all right?"

Libby forced a smile onto her face.

"Of course I am," she lied. "And don't worry, I'm just going to make myself a sandwich and then I'm coming up. I'll switch off the kitchen light and the hall light and the light in the family room…"

Mollie raised her hand and turned towards the stairs.

"OK, I know you are old enough to be responsible. I'll see you in the morning."

"Night," whispered Libby, as her grandmother's slight, upright form disappeared up the stairs, and it was all she could do to stop herself from racing after her.

As soon as she heard the water running in the bathroom Libby ran to the phone and dialed Amy's number. No answer. For a moment panic rose up inside her like a tide; then she heard the beep of the answering machine.

"Please leave your message after the tone…"

"Hi," her voice sounded stilted and she fought to calm it down. "It's Libby… just wanted you to know that I'm staying at Jack's tonight. Please call me. Something's come up again…"

If Amy ever got the message would she understand it, she wondered, and where could she be? Perhaps she really was ill.

The cinder pathway crunched beneath her feet as she walked

quickly toward the stone outbuildings, and her flashlight pinpointed a woodchuck scurrying through the long grass. Ahead of her the moon shone upon Jack's stable, and she could see his face, dark against its pale gleam. Was she doing the right thing, she wondered, or was she just overreacting? She hitched her bag further onto her shoulders and shrugged, clutching the wooden baseball bat she had found in her dad's workshop. If it was the Baker twins then they were in for a shock.

Jack nickered his greeting, obviously uneasy but pleased to see a friendly face.

"Don't mind me, boy," Libby told him as she slipped into his stable. "You get on with whatever you were doing and I'll just sit quietly in the straw here."

He stared at her, snorting gently, and she pressed her cheek against him, savoring the warm softness of his muzzle against her skin and the aroma of horse that filled her nostrils.

Half an hour passed. Jack, growing bored with her company, wandered back to his hay. Libby curled herself up into a blanket, reading a magazine in the light of her flashlight to keep herself awake, while outside the moonlit world was so still and silent that it seemed almost to be paused in suspense.

And then she heard the sound with disbelief; the soft crunch of feet on the cinder path, and as her flashlight fell into the straw a hand seemed to clasp around her heart, squeezing it so hard that her whole body began to tremble.

Chapter 9

The straw in Jack's stable glistened in the pale shaft of moonlight that fell across the floor, and Libby closed her fingers around the wooden baseball bat, gripping it so hard that her knuckles turned white and her fingers ached as she listened for the footsteps that were drowned out by the beating of her heart. They wouldn't get Jack this time without a fight, nothing was surer than that.

She clung onto the anger that flooded through her, flushing out the fear, and even gave her a deep-down flicker of relief as she realized that ghosts don't have footsteps. So, Jack's midnight exercise had nothing to do with the ghost of the long dead highwayman after all. Her anger swelled. She could cope with the living, but the very idea that those who once lived might still be hanging around after hundreds of years sent shivers of terror down her spine.

A shadow passed across the opening above the stable door, and she stepped forward, bat raised to strike. The minute anyone tried to open the door or even look over it, she would just hit first and think later.

"Libby… Libby…"

The hoarse whisper made her freeze, baseball bat hovering above her head. Was it a trick?

"Libby…"

It came again, and a warm surge of relief flooded her veins.

"Amy," she hissed. "Is that you? Here, come in, quick!"

Her friend's face appeared over the half door, a pale oval shape in the darkness, and Libby handed her the key and then waited impatiently as the padlock rattled.

When the door swung open and Amy's small figure was silhouetted against the moonlight, Libby felt that she had never been as happy to see anyone in her entire life. Grabbing Amy's arm, she almost dragged her into the stable and then went outside, fastened the bolts and padlock and clambered awkwardly back over the top of the half door.

"What was all that about?" murmured Amy.

"I don't want anyone to know we're in here," Libby told her, and in a low, hurried voice she filled her friend in on the events of that morning.

"Wow," cried Amy when she had finished. "Good job! I understood your message, but I can't believe that you were going to stay here all on your own. I had to wait until my dad went to bed; then I sneaked out."

The two girls settled uneasily down into the straw, jumping at every rustle from outside and clinging together in the darkness as midnight approached and the moon soared ever higher into the star-studded sky.

Libby hardly dared take her eyes off Jack, who appeared

to be totally oblivious to his mistress's fears. He stood rump towards them in the corner of the stable, one hind leg resting as he pulled at his hay, and as she studied the broad dark shape of his quarters in the semi darkness wild ideas kept coming into her mind. She tried to force them out, but they built up inside her head until she felt as if it were about to burst. At last, unable to stand it any more, she stood up and walked toward Jack.

"I'm going to sit with Jack until midnight," she announced determinedly.

Amy watched her, a puzzled expression on her face.

"What for?"

"Just a hunch," replied Libby. "If this really has to do with ghosts and stuff, there's something spooky about midnight, isn't there? I just think he'll be safer… that's all."

Amy giggled, a warm, normal sound in the eerie silence.

"You're crazy," she said, and Libby's teeth flashed white in the shadows.

"Oh well… here goes," she cried, clambering up into the manger to slide onto Jack's broad, slippery back. He flicked an ear back at her and heaved a deep sigh before going back to his hay net, and she lay down on his neck, placing her cheek against the silky hair of his mane. Amy watched uneasily, still convinced that the Baker twins were to blame and unwilling to allow herself to imagine even for a second that it had anything to do with the supernatural.

For several minutes Libby stayed prostrate upon Jack's neck, breathing in the scent of him as she listened to the crunching sound of his teeth upon the crisp seed hay, but then suddenly everything seemed to go hazy. She fumbled with her senses as if in a fog, trying to call out to Amy, but her whole body felt as if it were stuck in a mire of glue.

The rhythmic crunching seemed to become louder and louder, echoing in her ears, and then it mingled with another sound, a thundering sound, and she could feel a cool breeze against her cheek as Jack's muscles bunched beneath her. What was happening? She tried to call out to Amy but her mouth opened soundlessly and she felt her whole body spiraling upward, higher and higher, while below her Amy remained in the straw, totally oblivious to her plight.

Somehow they were galloping, headlong over a rutted track. Jack's breath was labored and his long mane, wet with sweat, lashed cruelly against her face. She wanted to scream, to cry, to yell at him to stop, but her whole body was out of control, stuck in the mire of glue and locked onto a pathway that could only lead to disaster.

It was she and Jack, and yet much more. One moment she was a part of him and could feel his body beneath her, straining with effort, groaning with pain, and then it was as if she were watching him from afar, a horrified and helpless observer as a huge figure drove him on, his whip lashing against her precious horse's delicate hide.

It was so real. The wind against her face, Jack's nostrils flaring red as blood against his black muzzle, and the man… the man whose face she could not see… the man who beat him into such a frenzied gallop that his breath came in huge, labored gasps, screaming in protest into the blackness of the night.

All thoughts of home and Amy were forgotten as she became a part of the moment, a part of the past, and a terrified and unwilling participant in the evil events that unfolded before her.

At last the thundering of hooves stopped and Jack stood motionless, head down, his flanks heaving as he fought for breath while his cruel rider sat heavy on his back, his cloak billowing out around him in the wind. And then he cursed loudly, hauling upon the curb rein so that Jack reared up into the air, his flailing hooves flashing as his shoes glinted in a beam of silver light.

"Stand and deliver!"

Along the road that wound toward them like a ribbon in the moonlight came a coach and four huge gray horses, eyes bulging with fear at the sight before them on the road.

"Stand and deliver," Jack's rider yelled again, waving something in the air. A pistol! He was carrying a pistol.

For a moment he half turned and Libby could see the mask of the highwayman covering his face as he stood his ground, but the driver of the coach and four leaned forward with a yell and flapped his reins, urging his mighty charges onward.

A loud crack rang in Libby's ears and the acrid smell of smoke filled her nostrils but her eyes were on the driver of the coach as he slumped forward, lolling like a rag doll over the side. Someone leaped from behind to take the reins and heaved the powerful horses to a halt, yelling at them to "whoa," and, as her heart pounded in her ears, they slithered to a halt, sides heaving and nostrils flaring in the moonlight.

The highwayman wheeled Jack around, the cruel curb rein hauling on his tender mouth, forcing him to rear again, higher and higher into the air.

"Your money or your life," he yelled, waving a second pistol, and when a face appeared over the door of the coach he rode along side.

"Out of the coach or you're dead."

There seemed then to Libby to be a moment of frozen silence, as the images around her etched themselves into her mind. Then came a flash of silver as the moon cast its light upon the barrel of a musket and someone yelled from behind the coach. The highwayman cursed as the sound of galloping hooves rose into the clear night air and two dark shapes appeared from over the hill behind them; two horses and riders, pounding along the ribbon of moonlight, intent upon justice.

The musket flashed and in the moment between the flash and the roar the highwayman fired, straight at the man whose horrified face peered over the door of the coach.

Libby felt something splatter against her, something warm and wet, and then somehow she was galloping again, the thunder of hooves taking over her whole being so that she became one with the horse that labored beneath her. She could feel the pain in his tortured muscles and the ragged gasp of his labored breath as his lungs began to fail, and in the moment before he fell she felt his awesome fear.

Something prickled Libby's cheek, and even before her eyes sprang open terror clutched her in its vice-like grip. Panic rose in waves through her body, echoed by the throbbing pain that wracked her muscles. It was a dream, just a dream, her mind told her. She was in that moment between sleeping and waking when the nightmare in her head was still so real that she trembled with the memory of it. And yet she knew that it was no dream.

"Are you OK?"

Amy's voice, so comfortingly familiar, brought reality back, and Libby clawed herself awake. Her face was wet, wet with the tears that ran soundlessly down her cheeks, and she rubbed her eyes desperately as if to try rubbing away the horrifying images that refused to go away.

"It was just a dream," she said out loud, but her heart screamed in opposition.

"What… you mean a nightmare?"

She covered her face with her hands, trying to control the erratic beating of her heart.

"Something like that," she whispered.

"Tell me," pleaded Amy. "What's going on? One minute I was watching you, and then you were sitting beside me crying. What's happened? I must have fallen asleep but I don't know how, because I was too scared to even *feel* tired."

Libby tucked her knees up to her chest, wrapped her arms around her legs and sat in silence for a moment, then she heaved a shuddering sigh and began to relive the awful nightmare while Amy sat beside her, listening in stunned silence as the tale unfolded. And when she finished, her voice breaking as she told how, in the final moment, Jack had collapsed beneath her, emotion flooded through her in an agonizing wave and she turned to look at Amy with desperation in her face.

"It was real," she sobbed. "It really did happen."

"It was just a dream," Amy told her calmly. "A horrible

94

nightmare, sure enough, but just a dream," and as if to prove her point she flicked on the flashlight and shone its beam around the stable. As it passed over Libby she gasped, bringing the light sharply back to rest on her cream sweater, and both girls stared in horror at the splatter of dark red that covered the pale material and dotted her face.

Libby reached down with one shaking finger and touched a crimson spot, holding the tip of it up to the light.

"Blood," she whispered. "It's fresh blood."

"There has to be an explanation."

Amy's jaw was set firm, but Libby shook her head, for in that moment she knew, with total certainty, that all her instincts were right. The nightmare was real.

It was Amy who rushed across to switch on the light. Desperate to bring some sense back to her friend she climbed over the half door and flicked the switch that she was convinced would reveal normality. The result brought a horror she could never even have imagined.

Jack stood at the back of the stall. His head was on his knees and his sides still heaved in agony as he fought for breath. His whole body was encrusted in a lather of sweat and his sides were marked with raised wheals from the highwayman's whip.

Libby ran towards him, fear forgotten as she ran her hands over his matted coat.

"We have to get him cleaned up," she cried, suddenly sure of herself. "We need warm water and a rug, and we'll make him a nice bran mash…"

"But won't the police need to see him as he is?" butted in Amy.

Libby paused, shaking her head at her friend.

"And what do you think would happen if we called them? What do you think they'd say when we told them that something or someone has taken my horse out without unlocking the padlock on the door and galloped it into the ground, and that I was able to watch the whole thing without moving from this place?"

"Or did you move?" murmured Amy. "And what happened to me?"

The two girls stared at each other for a moment, trying to fight off the raw panic that took their breath away and froze their limbs, and then Libby stepped forward.

"Come on," she insisted firmly. "Jack comes first. We're going to have to deal with this ourselves, but first we have to get him comfortable. You start brushing him and I'll go and get a rug and some water."

Amy hesitated.

"What if he needs a vet?"

A frown flitted over Libby's face.

"We'll worry about that when we've got him cleaned up, but I think he's just exhausted."

Half an hour later Jack looked like a different horse. Snugly wrapped up in a thick winter rug, he tucked into some warm bran mash with enthusiasm as the two girls looked on in relief.

"It seems crazy now, doesn't it?" murmured Amy, and Libby nodded.

"But it wasn't," Libby reminded her. "And we have to do something before it happens again, because next time Jack might not recover so easily."

"Yes, but what?"

Amy glanced at Libby, splaying her fingers helplessly and saw, to her surprise, that her friend's jaw was set and a fierce determination shone in her brown eyes.

"I don't know what to do about it yet, but I do have some ideas. Yesterday Gran's friend, Harry Redman, came for dinner, and he told me lots of stuff about Holly Bank."

Amy's eyes widened and she clutched Libby's sleeve.

"Tell me," she insisted. "Tell me everything he said."

As Libby related Harry's information about the highwayman who was supposed to haunt the cottage Amy felt a shiver rippling down her spine.

"It was the highwayman who rode Jack and held up the coach, wasn't it?" she whispered.

For several minutes the girls sat in silence digesting the awesome idea, and it was Amy who moved first.

"OK, then," she announced, standing up. "We'll go and see this Harry person today, and when we've got all the details we'll just have to find out how to exorcise the ghost."

"As simple as that," remarked Libby with the flicker of a smile.

"As simple as that," finished Amy. "Come on, I'll have to sneak back into the house before my dad realizes that I've been out all night. Then we'll go to Broad Oak."

Libby gasped.

"You must be joking! Broad Oak, today?"

"We have to behave as if this is just an ordinary day," insisted Amy. "And we can hardly go to see your Harry Redman at eight o'clock in the morning, can we? So we

97

might as well make ourselves useful. Anyway, it will take our minds off it, and as I have to see to Poppy anyway, you may as well help out in the yard."

"And when we've finished we'll go and find out the truth," finished Libby.

Amy nodded.

"Yes," she said. "And sort it out, once and for all."

"Once and for all," echoed Libby, wishing the horrible queasy feeling at the top of her stomach would go away.

As they walked back to the cottage a sliver of pink appeared over the horizon, heralding the approach of the new day. Libby clutched Amy's sleeve.

"He'll be all right now, won't he?" she said. "Now that it's light."

"He'll be fine," reassured Amy. "I'd turn him into the orchard if I were you; that will do him as much good as anything."

She clambered aboard her bike, foot poised on the pedal, and just for a moment Libby stood in front of her, reluctant to be alone.

"Did it really happen?" she whispered. "Or was it just a dream?"

A shadow fell across Amy's face.

"The blood is real," she said quietly, staring ashen-faced at Libby, and then suddenly she gasped.

"It's gone," she cried, pointing toward her sweater. "It was there… I saw it… I touched it. It was there and now it's gone."

Libby made a low moaning sound.

"Maybe it was never there… maybe it really was all just a dream."

"What?" snorted Amy. "The mud all over both of you. Was that a dream as well?"

For a moment the two girls just stared at each other.

"Well, one thing's for sure," announced Amy with such determination in her voice that Libby felt a surge of relief. "We are going to find out."

Chapter 10

It seemed strange, thought Libby, to be biking to Broad Oak as if it were just another ordinary day, when her whole world had just been turned completely upside down. She leaned her bike against the wall on the left of the main gate, walked across the deserted yard, and paused to listen to the low hum of voices that floated out from the feed room window, and then she headed toward the sound, eager for human contact.

When she pushed open the door and stepped inside the enticing aroma of horse feed met her and she took a big deep breath, reveling in the sheer familiarity of a morning at Broad Oak. Ancient ghosts and long dead highwaymen seemed a million miles away, but still she ran her fingers over her cheeks in a compulsive self-conscious gesture, as Jenny Harris glanced across in her direction.

"Morning," she called.

"Morning," echoed Libby hesitantly, wondering if Jenny could tell.

The cream sweater had gone straight into the trash, even though there were no longer any vivid telltale red marks. She had stared at it, searching for the faintest stain and unsure of whether she wanted to see one or not. The bloody marks had persuaded Amy that her experience was real, but that reality was just too hard to take. And Libby's face! Her fingers kept going back to touch her cheeks. Even now, when she had scrubbed the tender skin until it was red and sore, she couldn't help feeling that the marks were still there, ingrained into her for everyone to see. The thought made her flesh crawl but they were gone now, that was the main thing; that was what she had to cling on to.

When Mick came racing toward her with his pink tongue hanging out and a smile on his happy little face, she was glad of the distraction and crouched down onto one knee to give him a cuddle.

"Hello, boy," she cried, casting a surreptitious glance across to where Marcus was mixing feed in a purple bucket while Jenny doled out oats and mix and sugar beet. She felt uncomfortably aware, by the way their chatter had stopped mid-sentence when she walked in, that they had been talking about her, and a flush crept over her face. They couldn't know, surely they couldn't know, and for the hundredth time her fingers touched her cheek. Did she look different?

Marcus just grinned, a wide, innocent grin, and raised a hand, thick with the sticky feed.

"We were just talking about you," he said. "… I was telling Jenny what a terrific jumper your Jack is going to make."

Libby forced a smile onto her face. Everything seemed so alien after last night that she felt as if she was just acting a part.

"Thanks, I hope you're right."

She lowered her eyes, unable to meet his gaze.

"Do you want me to take some feeds out?"

Marcus frowned.

"Are you all right?" he asked with genuine concern, and she smiled again, a wide mechanical smile, then turned away abruptly.

"I'm fine," she insisted picking up the purple bucket. "Is this Flipper's?"

Jenny stood up with one hand on her back and ran the other through her hair, leaving bits of feed in her bangs.

"Oh, yes please," she said. "And will you take that yellow one for Moses as well?"

Libby eagerly picked up both buckets and made her escape, but as she walked out into the yard, to her dismay, Marcus fell in beside her.

"Come on," he insisted. "Tell me what's wrong," then he grinned and gave her a gentle push.

"Has that ghost been acting up again?"

Libby froze, her heart beating erratically inside her chest.

"Because if it has," he laughed. "I know how to sort it out."

She forced herself to walk on again. Did he know? How could he know?

His eyes lit up with mischief and she heaved a sigh of relief.

"My mother had an old friend around for supper last night," he told her. "And he seemed to know all about this area, so I asked him if he had heard about the Holly Bank ghost."

He paused then, waiting for her reaction, and she tried to

102

meet his gaze with feigned amusement, while all the time her teeth felt as if they were clamped so tightly shut that her jaw would never open again and all her nerve endings were screaming.

"And?" she eventually managed.

"And," Marcus went on with delight. "He said that the holly trees were supposed to have been planted to keep the ghost away."

A peculiar dizziness came over Libby as she remembered the sawn off stump near the stable.

"And did he say anything else?"

Her voice sounded distant, the voice of a stranger, but Marcus didn't seem to notice.

"No," he replied, disappointed at her seeming lack of interest. "Not really."

For a moment he held her gaze, and the dizziness seemed to spread down her arms, making her fingers tingle. Then his eyes crinkled into a smile and his teeth flashed white against the tan of his skin.

"Anyway," he went on. "At least now you know you're safe, because there can't really be a ghost at all, can there, not with all those holly trees to protect you."

Libby didn't know how she managed a light-hearted laugh. As if it was some kind of joke instead of a living nightmare.

"Thanks," she said. "That makes me feel a whole lot better."

"Libby," called Marcus as she started to walk away and she hesitated, looking back to where his angular frame was silhouetted against the sunlight. For once his expression appeared to be serious and she squinted her eyes to see him better.

"I really have only been winding you up about the ghost," he told her. "You're not really scared, are you?"

She let out a short explosive snort.

"Of course not… I don't believe in ghosts anyway."

It was almost lunchtime before she and Amy left for Harry Redman's house. First Mary Hunter persuaded Libby to hold the reins while she pulled one of the boarder horses' manes, and then Jenny insisted that they both help to bring some youngsters in from the far meadow. So it wasn't until they were biking down the lane that Libby eventually passed on Marcus's information about holly trees to her friend.

Amy's reaction was unexpected.

"That is the most ridiculous thing I have ever heard," she hooted. "I mean, I'm having trouble with the highwayman ghost thing already, and I'm certainly not going to start becoming paranoid about holly trees."

They rode then in silence, each deep in her own thoughts, and all the time Libby kept on hearing the awful crack and then the mournful rustling sound as the stricken holly tree crashed to the ground. She shook her head. This was ridiculous.

"It's just an old wives' tale, of course," she declared, pedaling furiously.

They passed the sign for Old Town village and headed toward the church.

"That must be Harry's house," she cried. "There, the one with the horse's heads on the gateposts."

They both stopped at the entrance to the drive, suddenly unsure.

"Do we really want to know?" asked Amy, and Libby shrugged.

"We have to know," she said.

The gardens on either side of the drive were beautifully tended and, sure enough, there was Harry Redman, his wild mop of gray hair lifting in the breeze as he busily hacked at a huge rose bush. He waved when he saw the two girls approach.

"Come on in," he called, beckoning to them. "I've got chocolate cookies and lemonade."

Libby was sure that she wouldn't be able to eat anything, but the cookies went down well, and she felt better when she had something in her stomach.

"So I suppose you two will be itching to know if I've found the book," said Harry with a smile, and the two girls nodded eagerly.

"Have you?" asked Libby.

His response was to stand up and usher them through an old oak paneled door into the hallway.

"I certainly have," he told them. "Come on, it's in the library."

The library proved to be a large book-lined room that had obviously once been very grand but now looked seriously neglected. There were books everywhere, on the floor, on the desk and even on one of the large armchairs that stood on either side of the ornate fireplace. Libby found herself wondering how he ever found anything, but suddenly there it was, right in the center of a large, leather topped, antique desk.

Myths and Legends of Old Town and Huttondale.

The title sprang out at her, and she felt herself begin to quiver in apprehension of what it might reveal.

"It looks very old," remarked Amy as he carefully turned the gold-edged pages.

"That's because it is," Harry told them, and then he paused, pointing at a headline with excitement. *The evil deeds of Black Jack.* That's him. That's your ghost. Now you two read the story while I go and finish pruning my roses."

The girls read avidly, their eyes devouring the pages, and as they read the blood in their veins seemed to become colder and colder.

Eventually Libby shivered, clasping her arms around herself.

"It can't be," she whispered.

"I'm afraid it is," Amy told her. "And it looks like there was some truth in what Marcus said about the holly trees as well."

"And Black Jack really lived at Holly Bank?" cried Libby, as if unable or unwilling to believe it.

It was Harry Redman who responded. He appeared in the doorway with a broad grin on his face, waving a pair of pruning shears as he shattered her world.

"He certainly did," he grinned. "I knew it would give you a shock. Just think of all the robberies he carried out from there, until the last one, of course. He galloped his poor horse ten miles that night, to hold up the coach on the great north road. No wonder the poor thing collapsed and died under him when he tried to make his escape. He should have guessed that such an important coach would have an armed escort."

"And they hanged him there and then," finished Amy.

106

"Well, they had to, didn't they?" remarked Harry. "He shot the Mayor of Lancaster stone dead and wounded the driver. They didn't mess around in those days, you know."

Libby sat down heavily into a chair. Her whole body felt numb. That was what she had seen, and if it happened again her beloved Jack... Fear bubbled up in her throat. Her beloved Jack might end up just like the poor unfortunate mount of that long ago highwayman. Each time he had been worse, had taken longer to recover, and perhaps next time he wouldn't ever get up again when he collapsed beneath his evil rider.

Harry Redman looked at her in concern.

"It's only a tale," he told her. "No need to be frightened. Anyway, you have the holly trees to protect you. That's why they were planted, you see, to keep him from ever returning to reenact his crime. Holly trees are supposed to have special powers, you know, and one of them is to keep evil spirits away."

"And do you believe it?"

Libby blurted the question out and Harry looked at her with a worried frown.

"I haven't frightened you, have I?" he asked, and she let out a high-pitched laugh.

"Of course not," she lied. "I just wondered what you thought."

"Well... "

He screwed up his face and scratched his head.

"I think anything is possible, and there are lots of things we don't understand, but I have never personally seen a ghost. Anyway..."

He grinned and ruffled Libby's hair.

"You have the holly trees to protect your home, so you don't need to worry."

The holly trees… the holly trees… they had to re-plant the holly trees!

Libby threw Amy a desperate glance, and as she turned toward the door the strange dizziness came over her again. She stumbled slightly and reached out for a moment to steady herself on the desk.

"Are you sure you're all right?" asked Harry, his face puckered in concern, and she managed a tight smile.

"I'm fine," she insisted as they walked back out into the hallway. "And thanks for telling us about our highwayman."

"Well, remember not to tell your gran that I've been frightening you," he called after them as they pushed their bicycles down the drive. "Oh! One more thing."

The two girls stopped and looked back towards him.

"Holly trees might keep evil spirits at bay," he told them. "But if you burn a holly tree it is supposed to summon them. So don't you two go setting fire to any bushes, will you?"

The girls cycled back towards Holly Bank in silence, trying to make sense of the things they had read. It was Libby who broke the brooding silence first.

"It said in the story that there was a full moon on the night the highwayman…!"

She paused, reliving the scene at the coach for the thousandth time.

"When his horse collapsed and died," she went on, and then silence fell again as she fought to put the rest of her thoughts into words.

"And each time Jack has been ridden in the night it has been around the time of the full moon," she eventually blurted out, closing her hand on the reins to allow Poppy to catch up.

There was a glimmer of hope in her eyes as she looked at Amy.

"So do you think it means that we have until the next full moon to find out how to exorcise his ghost?"

Amy shrugged.

"Maybe," she said. "I hope so. Anyway, there's only one thing we can do, so we may as well get on with it."

Libby felt as if her heart stopped for a moment and her stomach turned over.

"We have to replant the holly bushes."

Amy's jaw was set and her eyes sparkled with determination.

"It's the only answer," she agreed. "Whether we have until the next full moon or not, that is what we have to do as soon as possible."

Libby felt a new rush of confidence at her friend's determination, and a ray of hope brought a splash of color back into the blackness of her world.

"We'll do it as soon as we get back," she cried. "There must be plenty of holly bushes in the wood… or better still, I'll get my gran to take us to the garden center and we'll buy some."

To the two girls' relief Jack appeared to be almost back to normal when they approached the orchard. He was grazing on the rough grass around the trees and, at the sound of Libby's voice, he looked up and nickered gently.

His eyes were calm now, she noticed as she walked toward him offering a carrot, but traces of dried sweat on his dark coat brought the unpleasant memories rushing back as she slipped a leather head collar over his ears.

"You're going to be fine now," she promised, pressing her cheek against the warm silk of his neck, and then she closed her eyes tightly.

"Absolutely fine," she repeated. "Absolutely fine."

When they came to the holly stump he hesitated, shying and snorting softly. Libby looked determinedly away from it, but Amy paused for a moment.

"Do you believe it?" she asked. "About the trees, I mean… Or are we just scaring ourselves?"

Libby stopped and looked back, her brown eyes darkening almost to black.

"We have to believe it," she said. "It's Jack's only hope."

Chapter 11

Libby bashed her shovel against the rock again and again, determined to plant the tiny holly seedling they had found. Just one, that was all. After what seemed like hours of rooting through the undergrowth, it was the only holly tree they could find, or at least the only one they could dig up.

The sun was slipping over the horizon, time was running out fast, and one tiny plant couldn't possibly be enough.

"It's no good," declared Amy. "We'll just have to try and buy some bushes tomorrow."

Libby paused, shovel held aloft, and the flush brought on by all her efforts drained from her face, leaving it starkly white with just one red spot on either cheek.

"But what about tonight?"

Darkness loomed, bringing back all her fears.

"What if he comes back for Jack tonight?"

Amy reached out a hand and clutched her friend's arm.

"Look," she said. "We have to face facts; there's nothing more we can do until tomorrow, and anyway…"

She hesitated, trying to think of some way to appease Libby.

"If it isn't a full moon then he won't come at all, will he?"

"And it can't be a full moon again, surely," added Libby with the tiniest flicker of hope.

"What is all this talk about a full moon?" cut in a reedy, high-pitched voice, and the girls looked around with a start to see Mollie Blackstock's tiny figure standing behind them. Her hands were on her hips and her bright eyes glinted in the golden light of the setting sun.

"Someone called Margaret has been phoning for you since about four o'clock," she told Amy. "She said that you'd promised to be home early and when she rang Broad Oak they told her that you hadn't even been in to see to Poppy this afternoon. She sounded worried sick, and so I've been searching everywhere for the pair of you."

"We have to plant some holly bushes, Gran."

Libby's voice held such anguish that her grandmother's face softened.

"Well, you can't do it now – it's too late," she told her. "It's that Harry Redman, isn't it? I knew I shouldn't have let him fill your heads with all that ghost nonsense. Wait until I see him!"

"Don't blame Harry," pleaded Libby. "I was the one who insisted that he show us the book, and it's only local history, after all."

"History you can well do without," snorted Mollie. "I suppose you think that if you re-plant the holly trees they will keep the ghost of Black Jack away…"

"You know about Black Jack…?" butted in Libby.

"He is just a legend," said her grandmother. "An old wives' tale, but if you really are worried by Harry's stories

112

then I'll take you to the garden center first thing tomorrow and we'll buy a dozen holly bushes."

"I don't need a dozen, gran," Libby cried. "Just enough to replace the ones my dad cut down… And I need them now."

"I don't think one more night without those bushes is really going to matter that much, is it?" remarked Mollie firmly. "And you just wait until I get my hands on that Harry Redman, filling your heads with his crazy stories."

"Honestly, gran…"

Libby desperately pleaded the old man's case.

"This has nothing to do with him."

Shaking her gray head in exasperation, Mollie took a firm hold on her granddaughter's sleeve and urged her toward the cottage.

"Come on," she insisted. "Your supper will be dried to a crisp… And you, young lady…"

She paused for a moment to wave her other hand in Amy's direction.

"…You'd better get a move on, or I think we'll find your friend Margaret on our doorstep, probably with the police in tow… She really was desperately worried about you, you know."

"Was she… was she really?"

A smile lit up Amy's face at the thought, and Libby nodded knowingly.

"I said you should give her a chance."

"Maybe," she agreed. "Anyway, I'll see you first thing tomorrow, and make sure you call me if you need to."

"I hope she makes friends with Margaret," she remarked, as she watched Amy bike off down the lane.

Mollie nodded.

"It must be hard for her, I suppose, accepting someone new, but the poor woman really did sound genuinely concerned," she said, giving her granddaughter's shoulder a shake. "Just as I was," she reminded Libby. "Now come on inside and get something to eat."

Mollie was determined that evening to take Libby's mind off what she thought were her "silly fancies." She found a good movie on the television, all about a young girl who ran away to be a trick rider in the circus, exactly the sort of movie that Libby would normally have loved, but all Libby could think of was Jack, so alone and vulnerable in his stable.

To her relief the sky beyond the window remained totally dark, without even a single star to mark its velvety blackness. If Amy's idea was right, she realized, if the highwayman really only rode when the moon was full, then Jack was safe for now.

Her heart began to pound. But what if he wasn't?

It was almost half past eleven when Mollie finally went to bed. Libby pretended to follow her, then slipped quietly back down the stairs and out the back door. She would just stay with him until after midnight, she decided, just until she was sure that he was safe.

The door banged behind her, making her jump, and from somewhere close by an owl screeched. She clasped her hands over her ears and began to run through the darkness, tripping over tufts of long grass in her eagerness to make sure that Jack was all right. And then there he was, his head a darker shape against the shadows of the night as he watched her approach from over the stable door.

She didn't dare turn on the light in case her gran saw it, so she flicked on the flashlight and flashed it around the stable. He was safe… he really was safe. Relief flooded over her in waves and she quickly turned the silver key in the lock and slipped into the stable, breathing in the warm horsy aroma.

"It will be OK, Jack," she whispered, and he lifted his velvety muzzle to nibble her cheek. The gesture of trust brought a lump to her throat, and tears pricked the back of her eyelids.

"You'll see," she told him fiercely. "He won't hurt you tonight."

For an endless hour Libby stood beside her horse as he dozed in the darkness. She stared out into the moonless sky, reveling in its blackness as her mind went back again and again to relive the horrors of the night before. Her heart ached for the poor horse that galloped to its death all those years ago.

Long before dawn she crept back to her bed, content that Amy's theory was right; they had until the next full moon to plant the trees that would keep Holly Bank safe.

Her grandmother's voice woke her, calling urgently from the hallway, "Come on, love, rise and shine, Amy has been here for ages."

Libby leaped out of bed, disorientated, her head swimming as she dragged on her clothes. A splash of cold water against her face brought reality back and she hurriedly passed the toothbrush over her teeth and raced down the stairs two at a time. Amy flashed her a worried glance as she walked into the kitchen, but Libby's expression immediately relieved her fears and her features crinkled into a smile.

115

"Are we still going to get those holly trees?" asked Mollie Blackstock, piling toast onto a plate. "Or has a good night's sleep made you see sense?"

Libby smeared butter and jam onto the warm crispy bread and took a large bite.

"No…" she mumbled. "Now…" Then she swallowed and cleared her throat.

"Sorry, but I'm starving. What I mean is, please, can we go right now?"

Her grandmother glanced up at the clock.

"It doesn't open for at least an hour," she remarked. "So you may as well go and see to Jack when you've had your breakfast, and we'll set off at half past eight… And you, young lady," she went on, pushing the toast toward Amy. "Get yourself something to eat. I suppose you believe all these old wives' tales as well, do you, or have you more sense than my granddaughter?"

Amy giggled.

"Oh definitely," she replied, pulling a face at Libby. "A lot more sense."

The dark green leaves of the newly planted holly trees gleamed in the bright light of day, and Libby stood with her hands on her hips and a smile of satisfaction on her lips. The sentries were back doing their duty and Jack was safe again.

"Let's go for a ride," suggested Amy. "After I've been to see to Poppy, of course. I suppose we'd better do some work at the stables. I bet they're wondering where we've been."

116

"That," remarked Mollie Blackstock. "Sounds like a very sound idea, and I hope you have put all those silly fears out of your heads… Ghosts indeed. Whatever will you think of next?"

They ambled along the bridle path side-by-side, both contented with their thoughts and enjoying the feel of the sun against their faces.

"Of course we won't be sure until after the next full moon," remarked Libby, and Amy frowned.

"I never thought about that," she said. "You mean we'll have to stay in the stable all night again."

Libby nodded.

"I can't think of any other way to be sure."

"So how long have we got?"

"That," declared Libby proudly. "I *can* tell you, because I looked it up. There are approximately twenty-nine days, twelve hours, and forty four minutes between each *new* moon, so I suppose it will be the same for a full moon."

"Well, I think we should work out exactly what day it falls on and then try not to think about it again until then," decided Amy. "Or at least until a day or so before."

Libby nodded.

"I've already worked it out," she said. "It's the night before the qualifying show."

Their eyes held for a moment, and Libby shuddered, remembering Jack's very first show and his miserable performance. She still had guilt-ridden nightmares about the way she had made him jump when he was so exhausted.

"But what if it happens again?" she whispered.

"It won't," declared Amy. "I'm sure it won't… Not now."

117

Night after night over the next two weeks Libby slipped from her bed in the dead of night, making her way cautiously through the darkness to go and check on her precious horse. As the summer vacation drew to a close and the holly trees thrived she found herself beginning to relax. One more ordeal to get through. One more endless night in Jack's stable as the full moon rose in the sky, waiting for… It won't happen, she told herself firmly. Not now. And as the days slipped by her confidence grew and she began to focus more on the show ahead and put all her fears about the deeds of evil highwaymen behind her.

She spent hours schooling Jack, and as he gradually became more balanced and obedient her hopes of success secretly grew. Marcus turned up one morning when she was working him down a grid in the outdoor ring. He altered the jumps for her to help Jack get a better approach, and taught her to sit and wait for the fence instead of firing her horse at it. At the end of the session they walked back toward the stables together, and that was when he threw his bombshell.

"I see you've been planting holly trees," he remarked, one dark eyebrow raised.

Libby's mouth went dry and she shrugged.

"Just a few."

"So you *do* believe in the Holly Bank ghost after all."

He looked at her and she held his gaze, mesmerized by the expression in his eyes.

"I thought you said it was just a joke," she whispered.

"I *made* a joke of it," he remarked. "I didn't say I thought it was a joke."

They stopped simultaneously and Jack lowered his head to

graze while Marcus and Libby stood in silence, tension bouncing between them like a current of electricity. Then Marcus reached down to pick a yellow poppy and leaned back against the dry stone wall, picking off the petals one by one while Libby watched uneasily as they fluttered to the ground.

"My grandfather lived there when he was a boy," he eventually began, glancing at her to make sure she was going to take him seriously. Her face was white and set, and a haunted expression made her dark eyes look huge. Reassured, he went on.

"He told me a tale that gave me nightmares for weeks, and I never knew until this day whether to believe it or not. He kept his horse in the same stable where I presume you keep Jack, and he cut down the holly tree in the pathway."

A strange quiver ran through Libby, and she stared hard at the ground as he unfolded an all-too familiar tale of the horse being galloped into the ground, and an evil highwayman who robbed and murdered and met his untimely fate on a moonlit night.

When the last yellow petal fell onto the soft green carpet he handed her the poppy's naked stalk, and her voice trembled as she looked deep into his eyes and asked the question that hovered on her lips.

"And what did he do?"

"He replanted the tree."

"And the highwayman never returned?"

Hope sprang up inside her.

"He never returned," Marcus told her, gently taking hold of her fingertips. "So what do you know about it? Has it happened to you?"

119

Libby took a deep breath, her eyes half closed; it would be such a relief to tell someone who believed her… and yet. Her eyes sprang open. Could she really trust him… what if he was just making fun of her?

"But I thought you said it was your mother's friend who told you about the holly trees."

Marcus smiled, tightening his grip on her hand.

"That was just my way of trying to warn you. I didn't want to scare you, but I thought you ought to know, that's all."

Oh, how much she wanted to tell him. Her heart beat a staccato pattern inside her chest and her tongue seemed to stick to the roof of her mouth as his eyes bored into hers. Suddenly overcome by confusion she pulled her hand away and turned toward Jack; one day she would tell him, she decided… when she knew how he really felt about her… because for some reason that mattered so much.

"Come on," she said more sharply than she had intended. "Jenny will wonder where I went. I promised to help her with the three-year-old."

She pulled Jack's head away from the grass and set off along the path to the stable, dragging him along behind her while Marcus followed slowly. If she had seen the expression on his face as he watched her walk away, Libby might have realized exactly how he felt about her and reconsidered keeping her secret. As it was she turned her thoughts determinedly towards the future, and felt a glow of hope from somewhere deep inside. If planting the holly trees had worked for Marcus's grandfather… then it would work for Jack too. She was sure of it!

The next weeks seemed to pass so slowly that the two girls thought they would never be rid of the fear that still lurked inside them. The holly trees thrived, Jack stayed happy and calm and there was no sign of shadowy figures in the night or sounds of rasping breathing, however hard Libby tried to watch out for them. Gradually they began to relax, and when Libby brought Mick home to let him have a good sniff around the stable, he just wagged his tail disinterestedly. They finally began to believe that it really was all over.

"Well, this is it," remarked Amy, as show day loomed before them. "The very last lap."

Everything was ready for tomorrow. Poppy and Jack had been thoroughly shampooed, their tack soaped until it gleamed, and both the girls' jodhpurs and shirts were laid carefully across a chair in the corner of Libby's bedroom. Libby was standing at her window staring out into the darkening sky, and she turned at her friend's remark, her face white with tension and her jaw clenched.

"What do you mean by that?"

"You know what I mean," continued Amy. "After tonight it really will be over."

"You hope," snapped Libby.

"Look."

Amy stood up from where she was sitting on the side of the bed and walked across to stand in front of her.

"Being in a foul mood isn't going to help, is it?" she said firmly. "Last time you stayed in Jack's stable all night you went there by yourself. Tonight I'm going with you, so it can't be as bad this time."

Libby's face puckered up.

"Yes, but last time I didn't really know what we were in for. I mean, I thought that the worst thing that could happen was having to warn the Baker twins off."

"And this time *nothing* is going to happen," declared Amy. "So stop worrying and think about the show tomorrow."

A frown flitted across Libby's face. Then she smiled.

"Sorry, just nerves getting to me, I suppose. I know you're right. It's just…"

"Don't even think about it," warned Amy. "Less than an hour; that's all we need, just to midnight."

"Well, it's eleven thirty, and gran's gone to bed, so I suppose this is it," announced Libby, picking up her bag from the pile of clothes and discarded shoes on the bedroom floor.

"You were absolutely right about the full moon," whispered Amy as they stole silently through the orchard. It rose above them in the clear night sky, casting its eerie gleam across the earth so that the trees appeared to be etched in silver and the grass beneath their feet glistened. She hitched her bag further up onto her shoulder and crossed her arms, trying to control the shiver that prickled over her scalp.

"I thought you were the one who told me there was nothing to be scared of," smiled Libby.

Amy's fingers dug into her arm.

"That was when we were in your nice cozy cottage," she muttered.

Jack stared at his late night visitors with surprise, snorting softly.

"You'd think he'd be used to me creeping into his stable in the middle of the night by now," murmured Libby.

"Well, this will be the very last time, remember," hissed Amy as she slipped through the door while Libby refastened the padlock.

As soon as Jack was settled again they sat down in the straw, shoulders touching as they stared out over the half door at the luminous sky. Neither of them made a comment, but at five to twelve Libby climbed onto Jack's broad back and this time Amy stood close beside her, her fingers wrapped into his silky mane as they waited in frozen silence. And as the endless seconds turned to minutes and midnight came and went, Libby felt the fluttering in her heart beginning to settle. Yet still they waited, unable to believe that it really was over and Jack was safe.

At one o'clock Libby slipped to the ground. Her legs felt like jelly, and her whole body tingled with the awesome flood of relief that filled up her senses and left her feeling somehow weak and helpless.

"It's over," cried Amy. "Can't you feel it? It really is over."

Libby took hold of her friend's arm for support and laughed aloud at the shimmering moon.

"We've beaten you this time, Black Jack," she cried, and then she started to giggle, a low pitched gentle sound that rose and rose until it reverberated around the stable, and then Amy joined in and the giggle turned into a bellow of laughter.

"Come on," said Libby, wiping her eyes. "Let's go and get some sleep. We've got a big day tomorrow."

"The biggest," agreed Amy.

123

Chapter 12

Libby turned Jack to face the huge red and white brick wall and her mind went blank. She forgot to kick on, forgot to stay focused, and forgot the rhythm that had carried her successfully around the rest of the course. All she could see was the massive obstacle looming up in front of her. And then she felt Jack's shoulders bunch up and the incredible power beneath her as he left the ground. The crowd roared. For what seemed like an eternity they were suspended in the air, and then they landed with a lurch and somehow they were galloping around the arena, the spectators a colorful blur as Jack launched himself into a series of high-spirited bucks.

"Clear round," called the commentator. "In a time of 49.25 seconds, and that takes Libby Blackstock and Jack Flash into the lead."

After all the trauma of the last weeks, to Libby it seemed like an impossible dream. She kept thinking that she would wake up at any moment, but then she saw Amy's bright ecstatic face in the crowd and something warm melted her doubts.

"There's only one more horse to go," she shrieked. "You're going to qualify, I know you are."

Libby rode out into the collecting ring and headed her prancing mount across to where her friend was waiting for her by the ropes. The long suffering Poppy was quietly grazing beside her mistress as Amy jumped up and down, and Libby couldn't help but smile at her enthusiasm.

"There's still Jinny Longton to go," she reminded her. "And her horse, Cleo, jumped a clear first round."

"She won't be as fast as Jack though, you'll see," declared Amy with a confidence that Libby envied, and they both watched with bated breath as the elegant gray cantered through the entrance. Fence after fence flowed by as the talented mare sprang through the air, and Libby felt her mouth going dry as Jinny approached the final obstacle.

"Clear round," called the commentator. "Clear round for Cleo in a time of 49.5 seconds… and that makes Jack Flash the outright winner."

Libby's heart was thumping so loudly in her chest that she was sure everyone must be able to hear it. She had qualified for the finals at Stoneleigh next month; she really had qualified! Leaning forward, she patted Jack's damp neck madly as tears of joy dripped into his mane.

"Well done, Lib," cried Amy.

"Yes, well done," came a voice from beside her and Libby glanced up with surprise to see a slim blonde woman carrying two large ice cream cones."

"Now you've both won your classes," she declared, and Amy's face turned a deep pink.

"Margaret came to watch me in the Mountain and

125

Moorland," she said proudly.

"And you won?" shrieked Libby, feeling guilty that she hadn't already asked.

"Yes, she won," said Margaret proudly, and when she placed an affectionate hand on Amy's shoulder Libby felt a rush of delight flood over her.

She had been right about Margaret all along. Maybe now Amy could have a real family again. Everything was working out perfectly at last.

"I think they're calling you back into the ring," Margaret told Libby with a smile, and when Libby gathered up her reins and urged Jack forward he obliged with an excited leap.

"See you later," she called as he trotted through the entrance to claim his prize.

As she stood in the lineup, feeling so proud that she thought her heart might burst, with a sudden jolt Libby realized that Marcus was standing three horses down, mounted on his lovely gray. She had beaten Marcus Hunter. She looked around doubtfully as if expecting somebody to come along and tell her that it was all a mistake, but then someone was handing her a huge championship rosette and placing a sash around Jack's neck.

Pride swelled up inside her as she led the parade around the ring in a lap of honor to the sound of the band, and the whole crowd began clapping. Rising to the occasion, Jack catapulted into the air, and Libby stood up in her stirrups in an uncharacteristically impulsive gesture and punched the air.

The ride home was a euphoric amble, especially after Marcus came over when she was letting Jack graze after the class. He grinned, a slow, genuine smile of delight and held out his hand.

"Well done, Lib," he said quietly. "You deserved it... And you've laid your ghost to rest," he added in an undertone meant for her ears only.

His words kept going around and around in her head as she rode along the lane toward Holly Bank, and beside her Amy giggled and urged Poppy into a trot.

"Is it qualifying for the championships you are most pleased about... or being congratulated by Marcus Hunter?" she called, twisting around in her saddle to look back.

"Don't be so silly," retorted Libby, nudging Jack to catch up. "What do I care about Marcus Hunter?" she asked as side-by-side they headed for Holly Bank.

"A perfect end of a perfect day," sighed Amy. "And I'm glad that you told me to give Margaret a chance. She's not so bad, really."

As they rode through the entrance to Holly Bank they were met by an autumn smell, the acrid aroma of burning wood. A column of smoke spiralled way up into the clear crisp air and an unexpected prickle of apprehension made Libby's scalp tingle. She glanced at Amy, who was wrinkling up her nose in disgust, and then her vague fears suddenly fled as she saw a very familiar vehicle parked haphazardly across the driveway.

"That's my dad's car," she shrieked. "They're home! I can't believe it!"

"Well, you'd better believe it," came her father's deep voice, and there he was, standing on the pathway just ahead.

His arms were crossed over his chest, his cheeks were flushed with heat, and he had a pleased smile on his face.

"We got back early this morning just after you left, so as you and your gran obviously haven't touched the garden all summer I thought I'd better do a bit of tidying up before you came home."

He pretended to frown but his eyes crinkled with laughter.

"I don't know… what's a man to do? I go away to work and end up having to work as soon as I get home."

Libby looked past him to the column of smoke. For a moment she thought she heard a distant sound, like a thousand tiny echoes of a bygone, anguished cry and a cold hand seemed to clasp around her heart as she remembered Harry Redman's final warning.

"That old holly bush went up like a tinder box," announced her father, as thick clouds of smoke billowed out over the orchard. "Who would ever have thought it would burn so well?"